The Deadline

THE FRIESSEN LEGACY

THE FRIESSENS: A NEW BEGINNING
BOOK ONE

LORHAINNE ECKHART

The Friessen Family

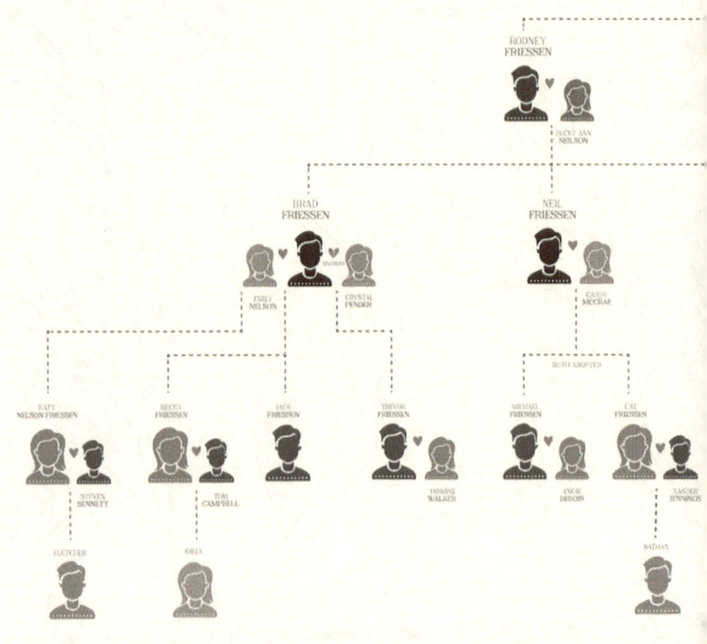

The Outsider Series

THE FORGOTTEN CHILD	BRAD & EMILY
A BABY AND A WEDDING	BRAD & EMILY & *and Jed and Neil Friessen & Candy*
FALLEN HERO	JED, DIANA & ANDY
THE SEARCH	JED, DIANA & ANDY
THE AWAKENING	ANDY & LAURA

The Outsider Series

SECRETS	DIANA & JED *with the series Friessen Family*
RUNAWAY	ANDY & LAURA
OVERDUE	JED & DIANA
THE UNEXPECTED STORM	NEIL & CANDY
THE WEDDING	NEIL & CANDY *and the entire Friessen Family*

The Friessens:
A New Beginning

THE DEADLINE	ANDY & LAURA
THE PRICE TO LOVE	NEIL & CANDY
A DIFFERENT KIND OF LOVE	BRAD & EMILY
A VOW OF LOVE	THE ENTIRE
A FRIESSEN FAMILY CHRISTMAS	FRIESSEN FAMILY

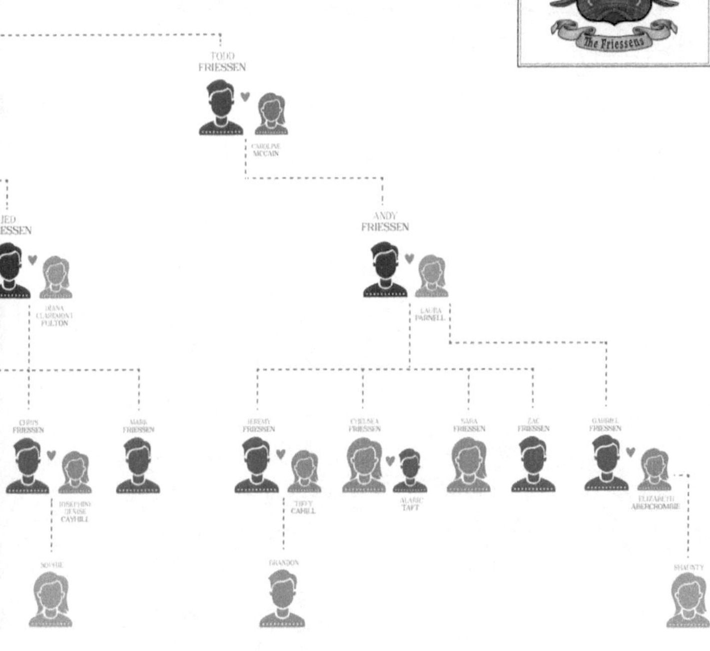

The Friessens

The Friessens

The Deadline

A husband moves to Montana to escape a deadly threat. But there's a new evil edging toward them. Can he save his family before it overwhelms them?

—*"Author Lorhainne Eckhart is adept at showing deeply felt emotions through actions, instead of just telling us. The insecurity, fear and paranoia practically emanated from Laura at the beginning of the story and watching her find her strength was truly an honor."*

REVIEWED BY NATASHA JACKSON,
READERS FAVORITE

—*"This book will steal your heart & have you waiting for the next one. It will also teach you to speak your mind when necessary. I do hope this situation never happens in real life! Don't miss a very good emotional read."*

WHODUNNIT, REVIEWER

—*"I love these Friessen men and their families. Was so excited the stories are going to keep on how going. Andy and Laura had a plate full with a sick child and moving to a new state along with twins. Andy has a strong personality and I appreciate him more after this book. What a man won't do for his family. Please read!"*

-JANET MURPHY, REVIEWER

In **THE DEADLINE**, Andy Friessen has packed up everything and moved his family two states away, to Montana, to protect his wife, Laura, his newborn babies, and his stepson, Gabriel, from the threats of his mother. What Andy doesn't know is that they'll soon face a new threat, one he never saw coming.

Gabriel is sick, and a trip to the doctor confirms Laura and Andy's worst nightmare: Without a lifesaving transplant, their son won't survive.

What Andy doesn't count on, as he tracks down the young man who fathered Gabriel, as well as Laura's estranged parents, is that a whole host of problems are about to be unleashed.

Chapter 1

How do you describe the feeling you get the first time you drive down a long, winding road to a place that is all yours? To Andy Friessen, this wasn't just a house or a piece of land: he had staked a claim in another state, in another part of the country, uprooting his family and selling everything, all for a brand new beginning.

Andy took in the miles of vast hillside and the cleanest pastures he'd ever seen. The green grass swayed in the wind and, for the first time, he sensed the sun, the moon, the stars and the changing of the seasons more deeply than he ever had before. This was a part of the country he had never travelled, but it felt like coming home. He glanced over at his wife, Laura, asleep in the passenger seat, her head resting against the door, her breath whispering softly in and out. He always knew when she was overtired, as she snored in her soft, delicate way. This time, she stirred a bit before settling into a deep sleep, as if her body had finally run out of steam.

She was on edge and had been for some time, but that

wasn't unusual for a mother of newborns. For Andy and Laura, there was twice as much stress with their six-week-old twins, Chelsea and Jeremy, who were sound asleep in the backseat of the truck. Their five-year-old big brother, Gabriel, Laura's son from a pregnancy at fifteen, sat beside them.

Laura was so young but had lived through more heartache, rejection and struggle than most people would in a lifetime. As a teenager, she had been tossed out onto the street by her judgmental parents, who thought she was a bad influence on her younger brothers. Laura had only mentioned it once to Andy, and only when he pushed. He wanted to know what had happened, to know everything about her family, but he saw the deep hurt like a tread mark on her soul. No matter what he did, he wondered if that was something she'd never be able to make peace with. Andy wouldn't, not in this lifetime. In fact, George and Sue Parnell were the first people Andy had ever hated without even meeting them.

They had come so far, Laura and him. At first, the only reason he had married her was to save her son when the state took him away. Laura and Gabriel had been living in her car, and Andy had married her because he felt responsible for the entire mess. After all, it had been his mother who fired Laura from her position as a maid in the Friessen house. Andy had treated her horribly at first, but so much had changed since then. He loved her—his child bride, as everyone teased him. She had recently turned twenty-one, legal in every state, and Andy would soon be thirty-three.

Andy pressed the brakes to slow his pickup as the ruts deepened on the driveway. The horse trailer rattled, and he glanced in the side mirror and rolled down his window just as his three-year-old buckskin mare, Ladystar, nickered. Apparently, she'd had enough of this two-day trip, leaving North Lakewood behind and moving two states away to a seventy-two-acre spread Andy had purchased outside of Columbia Falls, Montana.

"Where are we?" Laura said. She didn't open her eyes as she yawned. Her short bob was a tangled mess, but it was cute. Andy had been irritated when she cut off all her hair, saying it was easier to look after. Maybe so, but he liked her long hair. "Andy?" she said. The leather seat rustled as she sat up.

Andy had to clear his throat. "We should be close. …"

He stepped on the brakes when a sprawling one-story ranch house came into view. It had a light wood finish and a post-and-beam front deck, but something about the place didn't look right. The railing appeared broken, with pieces of wood scattered here and there. Everything looked unkempt. Piles of debris littered the yard, including a rusted-out pickup with missing wheels parked in waist-high grass that was now weighted down by the melting snow. Maybe he had the wrong place? He eased on the gas pedal and started up the slight incline that circled the house. It was similar to the photos he had seen, but the house in the photos had been newer than this. A couple of the shutters were hanging sideways, and the fence surrounding the house was falling down, as was the corral, but it was the junk, the debris, the plastic, garbage and scattered metal parts, that pissed him off.

"What the hell is this?"

He'd bought the place unseen. The Montana realtor had sent photos of the exterior and interior, and maybe Andy should have asked when they had been taken, but he'd been in a hurry to get Laura and the kids as far away from his family as he could. He parked in front of the house and spotted the red and white realty sign leaning against the front step.

"Andy, this doesn't look like the pictures the realtor sent," Laura said. "Are you sure this is the right place?"

One of the babies started fussing, and Ladystar nickered from the trailer.

"Andy, are we here?" Gabriel called out from the backseat, rubbing his eyes.

"Yeah, just stay there, bud," Andy said as he opened his door. Laura was reaching over to unbuckle Jeremy from his car seat, his tiny hands flailing. "He hungry?"

Laura appeared so tired as she nodded. "I think so. Wet, too." She patted his bottom and rested him on the seat. "Andy, can you reach the diaper bag on the floor in the back?" She had already unfastened his sleeper as Andy lifted the blue bag, shut the back door and set the bag on his seat.

"Just stay in here until I check things out," he said.

Laura glanced up with a weary smile. "Okay."

He shut the door and stepped around the truck, taking in the mess. Ladystar nickered again. "Okay, girl," he murmured, unlatching the horse trailer and leading his horse out before tying her to the side and bringing out a flake of hay for her. "Better find you some water, too," he said, pulling out his bucket. Around the side of the house, he found a barn with a missing door, another gated pasture, and a round ring. As he stepped closer, he noticed the round pen appeared intact, with no missing posts and all the rails up. It was probably a safe bet for tonight, at least for Ladystar, until he got a better look around.

He found a water tap at the back of the house and turned it on, but rusty water poured out. "Crap!" he muttered, waiting for it to run clear before he filled the bucket. When he took it back to the trailer where Ladystar was tied and eating, Laura opened the door of the truck and called out, "Andy, Gabriel has to go to the bathroom, and so do I. Can we go inside?"

Andy took in what was supposed to have been a ten-year-old sprawling rancher, with a wraparound deck where they could spend evenings and mornings looking out over their spread. Instead, it resembled the kind of house his cousin Jed would have picked up for a good price to gut and renovate—not something Andy was interested in doing.

"All right," Andy said. He opened the back door and lifted Gabriel, who was already unbuckled and waiting. "Stay here, Gabriel. Hey, Laura, Chelsea is still sleeping." Andy lifted his very quiet daughter from the car.

Laura slid down, carrying Jeremy, who was fussing again. She had on just a beige sweater. "Ooh, it's cold," she said. She reached in the truck for her jacket and pulled it out, holding it out to Andy so he could help her as she juggled the baby.

Laura started up the steps, and Gabriel and Andy followed. At the sound of a vehicle coming down the road, they both turned to see a newer pickup truck flying over the ruts and then pulling in just behind the horse trailer. A woman with a round face, bright smile, and dark hair tied back in a ponytail stepped out, wearing a sheepskin coat and blue jeans.

Laura shrieked behind Andy. He turned just as the screen door Laura had pulled fell over and crashed to the front deck. Chelsea, who had been sleeping, whimpered and then started howling along with her brother.

Chapter 2

"Andy, the door fell off!" Laura cried out.

"Are you all right?" Andy sounded worried as he set Chelsea's baby carrier on the deck and picked up the door, moving it over and leaning it against the house.

"Yeah, I'm okay," Laura replied. She was shaking as she clutched Jeremy, who was now crying louder. Her shoulder started to ache where the door had clipped her, and she must have pulled a face, as Andy was right there, setting his hand on her arm.

"You sure?" he asked. "Did it hit you or the baby?"

"Got my shoulder, but I'm okay." She loved it when he touched her, but right now she'd give anything for some warmth, her own home, and a hot bath.

"Looks like you got quite a mess here," the unfamiliar woman said, approaching with her gloved hand out. "Kim Edwards." She shook hands with Andy and then winked at Gabriel before taking in Laura and the two crying babies. "I saw you drive in. I live on the next property over.

Thought you might be lost or something, as no one comes out here."

"Andy Friessen, and this is my wife, Laura," Andy said. He picked up Chelsea's carrier and swung it a bit to soothe her. She loved being rocked in it, especially if it was her daddy doing the rocking. Laura was proud to be his wife, to be the mother of his children, and Laura wondered if she was lifting her chin higher at the sight of the strange woman. She also knew she'd never tire of hearing him claim her as his wife. "Unfortunately, I think I bought this," he added. "I need to have a word with the realtor."

"Who's the realtor?" she asked.

"Clayton Holmes. He came highly referred," Andy bit out.

Laura remembered all too well their original realtor, who had passed on Clayton's card. Now that she thought about it, Laura recalled their realtor might have mentioned he was family.

Kim winced. "Referred by whom?"

The way she said it had Andy taking on an expression Laura had come to recognize as a sign that he was digesting information and sifting it through his shrewd mind, deciding the best way to handle something. Unless someone knew him really well, they might think he was being rude by not answering.

This was a dark side of him that Laura knew all too well. He would protect his family at any cost; and she'd learned not to ask what he was thinking, because he wouldn't tell. His silence had been a source of many of their fights in the past.

"Good luck! You may want to make sure everything is where he said it is—if you can find him." Kim chuckled, but it didn't sound as if she found their predicament funny.

"What do you mean, if I can find him?" Andy asked with a bit of an edge.

"Well, last I heard, he left town, but then, I don't know for sure."

"Andy, I have to pee," Gabriel cried out, tugging on his jacket.

"Okay, come on, bud. Let's see if the bathroom works." Andy frowned and sighed as he rustled the doorknob. The locked door wouldn't budge. He shoved his hand in his pocket and pulled out a set of keys. "Well, let's see if these work."

He shoved one in the deadbolt and unlocked it, opening the door. The air that wafted out smelled stale and musty. Laura couldn't help but wrinkle her nose and cough. She must have pulled a face, as Andy said, "Let's open some windows." He took Gabriel's hand and stepped inside.

Laura glanced at the attractive neighbor. As always, around someone she didn't know, her mind went blank. She didn't have a clue what to say. That was where Andy excelled: he filled a room, he took over, and he led. He watched, studied, always knew exactly what to say; and he also never worried what people thought. Laura sometimes wished she could be more like him.

The woman rested a booted foot on the bottom step. "Can't believe someone actually bought this place. It's been empty for five years now," she said. She didn't smile, but her expression softened as she took in Jeremy, now starting to settle in Laura's arms. "You have your hands full —three kids, and twins. Where did you folks move from?"

Laura really wasn't comfortable talking to strangers about her business. "North Lakewood," she said. "Andy wanted a new start for us, so ..." She couldn't for the life of her figure out what to say that wasn't too private, like the fact that Andy's mother had tried to steal her babies and had even conspired with the doctor to perform a C-section and take them while Laura was sleeping. They couldn't prove any of it, even the doctor said it wasn't true, but Andy had decided to move them as far from his family's reach as he could. Laura wasn't about to share any of her secrets with a woman she barely knew, so the uncomfortable silence lingered.

She shivered, and Kim gestured to the door. "You should take that baby inside. It's still chilly here. I'm not sure what works or if any power is hooked up, though. Didn't see any utility trucks coming out this way."

Laura started inside and then stopped. She had to remind herself that she wasn't a rude person, but that was exactly how she was acting towards their new neighbor. "Kim, come in," she said. "I'm sorry, just tired from all the driving."

Laura could hear echoes from inside the empty house. She was in awe as she took in all the wood, the high ceiling, the big, open-concept front room, and the dust and cobwebs that were so thick they would take a cleaning crew a week to get through. There were two hallways, one at each end of the house, as well as a loft with a cathedral window. Laura flicked the light switch and the light flickered on. "There's power," she said before turning off the light again in the sun-brightened room.

"This used to be a beautiful house," Kim said. "The oldest son of the Miller family, who've been around these parts for many years, had this built for his wife. Can't remember her name... Claudia, that was it." She picked up a pile of papers and wood that had been left sitting by the woodstove and cracked open the glass door, looking in and pulling on the damper. "I'll get this going for you, warm it up in here." She loaded it up and pulled a pack of matches from her coat pocket. "Jeff Miller—he would be in his fifties now—came home one day and found his wife in bed with another man, her tennis coach, I think. Anyway, he shot him."

Kim glanced up at her, and maybe it was the horror showing on Laura's face that made her add, "Sorry, he didn't kill him, only wounded him. Jeff got time served for good behavior and put the house on the market. Claudia, I think she ran off with that tennis pro, or maybe it was a golf pro. Don't know for sure, but they left together as soon as he was out of the hospital, and this house just sat here with no one to look after it."

Laura watched her neighbor, still feeling the heebie-jeebies of being in the same house as someone who had almost been killed. She wasn't sure what she believed, but she also wasn't one to find out. She took in the sight of Kim as she got the fire going, so confident——just stepping in and acting. Laura couldn't do that. She felt awkward, and still worried about what others thought. Gabriel came running in, Andy behind him.

"Bathroom works," Andy said, gesturing down the hall. He looked up at the cathedral ceiling and then over at Kim before frowning at Laura, who shrugged. She knew why he was bothered—or she hoped she did, at least. Kim was starting a fire, warming his house, when Andy had two hands to do it himself.

Kim closed up the woodstove, the flames burning the dry wood as it crackled. She wiped her hands on her jeans and smiled brightly. By the tiny lines around her eyes, she was probably closer to Andy's age. "That should take some of the chill off," she said.

Andy started toward Laura and tilted his head. "Bathroom?" he said, holding his arms out to take the baby. Laura held tight even though she did have to go. Andy obviously hadn't picked up on her unease at leaving him with another woman—a smart, confident, good-looking woman. She was being ridiculous, stupid and jealous, but she couldn't help it. Andy was every woman's dream man.

"Laura, go," he said, taking the baby from her arms.

Laura didn't miss the puzzled expression on Kim's face before she brushed her slender, capable hands together and said, "Hey, listen, I should get going. I hope you don't stay here tonight. This place has been closed up a long time and needs a good cleaning."

"We'll make do," Laura said as she slid her hand over Andy's arm, making his dark leather jacket rustle. His eyes flashed at her and she wondered for a minute what he'd say. "The furniture comes today, doesn't it?" she asked.

"Sometime, but Kim's right——this place isn't ready. We need to get it cleaned first, and I need to have a talk with the realtor. I better be able to get a hold of him. Besides," Andy added, "I think we'd be better off in town tonight. I'll get a hotel for you and the kids, and I'll come back and get Ladystar settled."

Laura wanted to stay and argue, but she really did need to go to the bathroom; and the last thing she wanted was to have anything she said dismissed by Andy in front of this woman. That was just something she couldn't tolerate, so she turned and headed down the hall, taking in the open doors, the bedrooms, and the one bathroom with a nice round tub, a separate shower, and a sink that dripped and dripped. She listened with one ear to her husband as he had a conversation with the new lady neighbor, who was pretty, confident and capable—absolutely everything that Laura knew, deep in her bones, she wasn't.

Chapter 3

Andy stared out the window, watching as Kim drove away. Jeremy was fussing a bit in his arms when he heard the bathroom door open, and Laura stepped out. Gabriel was sitting quietly by the fire, which was unlike him.

"Hey, bud, you okay?" Andy asked. Gabriel shrugged and didn't say anything.

"What's going on?" Laura asked, hunkering down behind Gabriel, who was still bundled in a black down coat. She frowned, resting her hand on his forehead. "He's hot." She glanced up at Andy, who didn't miss the worry in her expression.

"Gabriel, are you feeling sick, buddy?" Andy asked.

"I'm tired and I'm cold," he muttered, whining against Laura.

"He slept most of the way here. Maybe he has the flu," Laura said. She had been ready to demand they stay here, throwing down a mattress and some blankets on the floor, but maybe that wouldn't be such a good idea with Gabriel sick.

"Here, take Jeremy," Andy said. "I'm going to get Ladystar set up in the round pen and then I'll get us a hotel room in town, just until we can get this cleaned up and I can find out what works and what doesn't. I need to get a hold of that damn realtor."

Laura started to stand up, but Gabriel wouldn't let go of her arm. He just whined and moaned. "Gabriel, here, lie on my coat," she said, shrugging out of her white down coat and laying it on the floor. Gabriel curled up on his side and faced the fire.

"Here, take him." Andy handed Laura the baby and shrugged out of his coat, slipping it over her shoulders just as Chelsea starting fussing from the carrier against the wall. When Laura tried to lay Jeremy on the floor beside Chelsea's car seat, he started howling.

"Andy, help me for a minute. Just let me feed Chelsea."

He wiped his face, glanced out at Ladystar and then unbuckled his baby girl. "It's okay, Chels. There's my girl." He kissed her chubby little cheek just as Gabriel started crying. It was one of those moments where Andy had to take a breath and remind himself that the kids came first.

An hour later, Andy was leading Ladystar into the round pen after walking around and checking the soundness of the rails. He had just latched the gate when an older model, green SUV pulled in, and out stepped a slim man in dark glasses and a cowboy hat, wearing a heavy sheepskin coat.

"Hey," Andy called out as he latched the gate, setting the halter and lead rope over the railing.

The man started walking towards Andy and raised his hand up. "You Andy Friessen?" the man asked, digging into each step.

"Yeah, and who're you?" he asked as the man approached and extended his hand.

"Bill Mansfield, with Sommerhill Realty. I got a call from Kim, your neighbor. She said you folks were using Clayton and bought this place."

Andy shook his hand. The younger man looked as if he'd just started shaving yesterday. "So tell me, Bill, where is Clayton?"

"Took off. Cleaned out the petty cash, too. Left quite a mess, really, on some of his deals, yours included. We came across your file yesterday and tried to call you, but your phone was disconnected."

"My home phone was. My cell phone works just fine," Andy snapped. "So what are you saying? I can assure you I bought this place, got the legal papers and everything to prove it."

The man backed up. "No, that's not what I meant. You do own it. That much is done. It's just that, well, what we found is that Clayton may have fudged some of the details."

Andy shoved his hands in his coat pockets and glanced around. The photos of the place had boasted a post-and-beam barn, fenced pastures, a sprawling rancher, everything new. "'Fudging' sounds to me like a fancy word people use for lying, scamming, and cheating. So what did he lie about, exactly, other than the fact that the house isn't new? The place seems to need repair, and that's just from what I've seen in the first ten minutes of being here."

"Yeah, well, there is that," Bill said. "The photos were taken when the house was first listed five years ago, but no one has been living here to take care of the place. The owner is gone——and there was the scandal with his wife, but you don't need to hear about that."

"Then tell me what I do need to know, other than the fact that someone owes me some money," Andy barked. He was ready to take a strip off this realtor.

"Now, hang on a second. I'm here merely as a courtesy —and because Kim called. I'm just trying to be a good neighbor and help out. Clayton was an independent realtor. He didn't work for anyone, and he's responsible for his own clients."

"Nice," Andy muttered. He looked away, unable to believe how he'd been duped. He was the shrewdest business man there was, and he sure as hell wasn't about to admit that he hadn't done his homework. He knew he should have hired an independent guy to come and inspect the property, but he had been in a hurry to get his family ——his kids, as far away from his mother as he could. He'd been distracted, sloppy, and he'd kick his own ass if he could. "So tell me, how much did I overpay for this? It is seventy-two acres, right? That's what the deed says."

"Yes, seventy-two and a half, to be exact, but the assessment value was fudged to the tune of three hundred thousand, we believe," Bill said.

"The spec sheet I received on all the features, was that fudged, too?"

"From what we can tell, we think so, but you should go through it and double check. You've got in-floor heating … here, let me see." Bill reached into his inside pocket and pulled out a couple sheets of paper. "As you can see, we marked off everything we know is correct from the seller. The Miller family are good people, and this is a class-A dwelling. Most of what you see is just from the lack of upkeep. It shouldn't take much to straighten the place out."

"Really?" Andy said with a hint of sarcasm, looking around and wondering what this kid was talking about. "I have a wife, twin babies, and a sick little boy, inside a dirty house that will take an army to clean. I've got pastures here with downed fences almost everywhere, the barn door is falling off, and I haven't even checked——"

"That's why I'm here," Bill interrupted. "I'll get someone out here to clean the place up for you. I felt bad when Kim called and told me how bad it was. We're neighborly folks around here, and I'm doing this to help out."

Andy didn't have a chance to say a word before he heard the moving truck pull in, carrying all the furniture he hadn't sold off. "Well, you better call that cleaning crew now," he muttered, starting back to the house to deal with yet another mess.

Chapter 4

"Look, this is just for the night." Andy closed their hotel room door, setting the baby bassinets on the bed. This had been the only room available, with two queen beds and a pullout sofa. Laura had tucked Gabriel into one of the beds and he'd fallen asleep as soon as she took off his shoes, but Andy was worried as he glanced over at their son. Laura was nursing Chelsea, and Jeremy was lying on the bed beside her, kicking up his legs.

"How's he doing?" Andy slid his coat off and dumped it over their luggage.

"He just wants to sleep, Andy. I tried to get him to drink some water," Laura said.

Andy nodded. "Let him sleep. Hopefully, he'll be better in the morning and these two won't pick up whatever bug he's got."

The last thing Laura wanted was two babies sick along with Gabriel. Flu bugs and colds generally went through the entire house, taking them all down one by one. The fact was that Laura was so damn tired that her bones ached. Getting up twice a night to feed the twins was starting to take its toll on her. On the bed beside her, as if reading her thoughts, Jeremy started fussing, cramming his fist into his mouth.

"Andy, I don't know how much longer I can nurse these two," Laura said. "When I feed one, the other needs feeding, and then they both need to be changed and …" She glanced up at him and felt bad immediately. "I'm sorry. I didn't mean it. I'm just tired."

"I know you're tired," he said, picking up Jeremy. "Hey there, what are you doing, giving your mama a hard time?"

Every time Andy held one of the babies, it tugged on a spot in Laura's heart. He loved them so deeply, and he was an amazing father. He'd never allow anything to happen to them. At times, Andy could be over the top; so strong and so unbending. She may have once doubted his love for her, but never for the babies——not even for Gabriel, who wasn't his biological son.

"I'll get Chelsea and Jeremy bathed. You get some rest," Andy said.

"I'd love to have a hot bath," she said, putting it out there for him.

Maybe Andy took that to mean something else, as he sat beside her on the bed, sliding his arm around her. "Maybe after I get these two down, I'll join you," he said.

After all, it had been a while since they'd made love ——before the twins, and Andy was not a man to wait. He was hot blooded and so male, but he'd been patient. Whatever opportunity there had been, well, she'd fallen asleep. They'd had nothing more than a chaste kiss here and there; a touch, a caress, right before one of the twins cried out or Gabriel raced in. They needed privacy and time, after she was rested. Right now, she had a choice between loving her husband and letting him do all those wonderful things that had her screaming out his name as he filled her over and over, or wrapping her arms around her pillow and falling into a deep sleep. Well, it was the pillow that won right now, hands down. She wondered if other women felt the same way she did. She heard that marriages often went through a rough patch after kids——and now she understood why.

Chelsea slipped off her breast, and Andy's eyes went right there. They exchanged babies, and when Jeremy latched on to her other breast and started suckling, she leaned back against the pillow and closed her eyes for just a minute. The next thing she knew, Andy was taking Jeremy from her and tucking her in bed.

Chapter 5

"Everything's loaded up," Andy said as he strode into the hotel room. Laura was bundling up the babies and buckling them into the carrier. Gabriel was still lying on the bed, bundled in his coat, his pajamas on underneath. He still hadn't shaken off the flu bug, but hopefully he'd start to feel better once they were settled in the house. "You ready yet?" Andy said. "I want to get there while it's still early enough to do something."

He realized it had come out a little sharp, as Laura flinched and hesitated before setting the buckle in place over the twins. Andy ran his hand over his face a couple times to try to ground himself.

"Why are you so irritated this morning? Did I do something?" Laura asked, sounding genuinely hurt.

Andy groaned. He really didn't want to get into this right now. "You've been really tired lately," he said.

"Yes, of course I have. I feel like a damn dairy cow. How many times am I up at night, feeding the babies—— and during the day? If they woke up at the same time, I would be getting more sleep. But right now, I get one down and the other one wakes up. I'm sorry, Andy. I'm doing the best I can," she said.

Well, now he felt like crap. Laura was all but falling over with exhaustion, and it didn't help that he wanted to paw at her like some randy teenager. If he didn't do something about this soon, the tension between them would ramp up and the distance between them would grow. The fact was that he needed her. "Okay," he said, holding up his hand as if letting her know he'd decided what they needed to do. "First things first, we get settled in the house. Then, I'm going to hire help for the kids."

Laura's expression took on a hurt he hadn't seen in a long time. Along with being tired——she was misunderstanding everything he said. "I'm not irresponsible, Andy," she snapped. "I'm capable of looking after my own children."

Yeah, she had definitely taken it the wrong way. He took a step closer to her, then another step, until he had backed her against the wall. He traced his thumb over her lip, her cheek, sliding his hand into her hair, taking in her startled green eyes. The weariness that had been there a second ago was now replaced with surprise, and he stepped closer still, pressing into her with all his hardness. Her breath caught. He rubbed his nose against hers, his warm breath fluttered across her lips, and her tongue flicked out and over her lower lip. He was so close to her, almost touching her, that she wrapped her arms around his neck, trying to pull herself closer. He started to lift her and was about to strip her right there when the baby squealed. He nearly dropped her, stepping back quickly and glancing at Gabriel, who was still asleep on the bed, his back to them.

"Oh my God. What the hell was I thinking?" he said.

Laura was standing there, dazed, and he wondered if the hint of pink on her cheeks was the start of a blush. She slid her hands through her short hair but didn't say a word as she stared at him, licking her lower lip again. Did she have no idea what she did to him when she looked at him like that? His eyes went instantly to her lush tongue, and his thoughts went running to images of his own tongue over her sweet lips, tasting her. Her eyes widened as she took in his arousal. He couldn't hide it, which only added to his agony.

"Andy, the kids …" she started.

"We're hiring help for the kids so you can get some rest," he began, stepping toward her again, closer. He knew she understood his meaning. "If I don't get my wife back soon, well, let me be clear——my mood is unlikely to improve. I want you willing, rested, and an active participant when I have you under me again." He set his hand around her chin and pulled her closer, nipping her lower lip between his teeth and kissing her deeply before stepping away. "Understand?"

She was out of breath. She swallowed, her cheeks flushed. "Yes."

"Good," he said.

Chapter 6

Before she opened her eyes, she could smell him, and her body became aware of his heat beside her in bed. He was all lean, hard—a work of perfection. She loved to wake up in the morning, tucked up against him, skin to skin. She slept with her head on his shoulder, which was hard as a rock, but to her it was the perfect pillow. When he rested his arm around her, his hand on her hip, holding her possessively against him, Laura was positive she had died and gone to heaven. Andy would never let her wear anything to sleep, as he himself always slept naked.

"Good morning, sleepyhead," Andy whispered as he nuzzled her ear, lifting the hair from the back of her neck and kissing her.

She didn't want to open her eyes—not yet, anyway. She wanted to lie there and feel all the delicious things he was doing to her body. He was amazing, how he loved her. He could have her doing anything for him. "The kids awake?" she asked. Her voice squeaked as he ran his hand over her stomach and touched her sensitive breasts, jolting her as if with electricity. She had been so exhausted for so long, but now he ignited her desire.

Andy hadn't found her any help yet, but he'd stepped up to the plate, helping more than he usually did——allowing her to nap and rest. Chelsea and Jeremy had also decided to get their timing down, and they had woken up only once the past night.

"Don't jinx it. We need to hurry, before they wake up," he said. He rolled her over on her back and was between her legs. "I can't wait long. I'm sorry."

She didn't want to wait either, and she ran her hand over and down his back. He slid his hand between them to touch her, and she thought she would come off the bed from that simple touch. He rubbed his nose against her, touched her lips with his as he slid inside her slowly, taking care not to hurt her. He held himself above her and watched, his eyes taking on a heat she hadn't seen in so long. Then he moved.

"Are you okay?" he whispered, his voice close to the edge. She could feel the way he was holding himself back, as he moved again.

"Yes. Oh God, Andy." Her voice squeaked, and she could feel his strength with every move as she ran her hands over his back and wrapped her legs around his waist. It felt like an eternity since they'd been this close, and the rush didn't lessen the magic that had always been between them. Maybe because they hadn't connected this way in so long, Laura lost all ability to reason—caught up in the insanity of the moment. She was about to scream out when she heard one of the babies cry, and Andy exploded inside her, filling her with warmth as she joined him—rushed, hurried, and amazing.

He didn't stay inside her but pulled out, leaving her feeling cold and empty. She loved it when he lay with her after, staying inside her until she felt all her senses return. Instead, he slid out of bed and walked naked, comfortable with his amazing body, comfortable with who he was. She wondered if he ever questioned for a second who he was and what he needed to do. She openly studied his body, all lean and solid, with dark hair lightly covering the most amazing chest and six-pack abs. Even with the cut of his muscles across his shoulders and back, the man had it all going on.

Laura started to get up, but Andy stopped her, pulling on a pair of jeans. "I'll get Chelsea before she wakes Jeremy up," he said. He had just zipped up when Jeremy let out a howl as if he had just realized Chelsea was about to eat without him. Andy added, "Well, why don't I get both of them?"

Laura smiled as she heard Andy through the baby monitor, listening to how he talked to his babies. He loved them so much, and she beamed, thinking of what an overprotective father he was. He changed the babies' diapers and brought them in for Laura to nurse in bed as she relaxed—still feeling the effects of Andy loving her. It had been so long, and she had now realized just how much she needed Andy's closeness, just as much as he needed her.

They still had boxes piled everywhere. It had only been two days since they arrived, and they still had a lot to get through, but the cleaners had transformed the house into something closer to the pictures they'd originally seen. The place had five bedrooms and three bathrooms, with a formal dining room, a bright, spacious kitchen with two built-in ovens and a gas range, and there were three fire-places throughout the house, with a huge walk-in closet in their master bedroom. However, Laura thought the best feature was the sunken tub in her bathroom—the huge plate-glass window revealing a view of the distant mountains.

"Laura, you should slip into the bath and relax a bit after you finish nursing the kids," Andy said. He had that very male look of a man who took pride in his woman. Just watching her care for his babies seemed to inflate his ego.

"Did you check on Gabriel, see how he's doing?" Laura asked as he made no move to leave.

"He's still warm, but he's sleeping. I'm going to make some calls—see about getting him a doctor's appointment." Andy stepped inside the bedroom and added, "I'll just grab a quick shower first."

An hour later, she lounged in the bathtub and listened to Andy in the other room, the babies cooing. When Jeremy started to fuss again, she felt the familiar pull in her breasts. How could he be hungry again? He ate way more than his sister and was packing on the pounds faster than she was.

So much for a break. The water hadn't even had time to cool, but she drained the tub and quickly dried off, pulling on her robe and striding out to the living room, where boxes were still piled. Andy was wearing a long-sleeved dark shirt tucked into newer blue jeans. He rummaged through one of the open boxes on the table, pulling out papers while holding Jeremy, who had crammed his fist in his mouth and was sucking away. Andy turned her way and did a double take, his eyes flaring as he took in the sight of her. His expression was approving and intimate—at least she thought so, anyway—and he winked.

"You look better," he said.

"I feel better. Thanks for letting me chill out in the bath for a bit. I feel … refreshed." She walked up to him and slid her hand over his arm, feeling the cut of his biceps.

She loved how he kept himself in shape...really good shape. He was tall, handsome, strong: a man who could take on the world for her and protect her and the children, but only if she trusted him. She'd learned long ago that Andy could be difficult and stubborn, but he'd always do right by her, by Gabriel and their babies. Trust was something he expected and didn't take lightly, nor did he give it easily. Because everyone had let her down in the past, Laura looked for every reason not to trust him. She wondered, would she ever be able to let that go?

"I'll take him," she said. "Not much you can help him with right now."

Andy leaned down and kissed her. "He's eating an awful lot again."

"Well, I'm starting to think he wants to use me as a pacifier. Gabriel still sleeping?" Laura looked around the living room and glimpsed Chelsea, who was in one of the baby swings, fast asleep. Gabriel should have been running around, but he'd been in bed ever since they moved in. Laura couldn't believe the flu had taken her son down this quickly. She was starting to worry—his fever was still high and he'd barely eaten anything.

"Yeah, he is," Andy said, sounding worried. "I called Kim and asked for the names of local doctors. She gave me a few, but there's only one pediatrician in Columbia Falls. The office should be open now." He glanced at his watch.

"What time is it?" she asked, settling into the corner rocker as the baby latched on to her breast.

"After nine," Andy said.

"Andy, Gabriel's never been sick like this before. I'm starting to worry. He won't eat—he drank a little apple juice with water, but he's so little, and his face seems thinner. This just isn't like him."

"I know, Laura, but kids do get sick. Let me call and we'll take him in. We'll have the doctor check these two out as well, since we're there."

Andy dialed the phone they had hooked up the day before and then stepped into the kitchen, where she could hear him talking. He reappeared a few minutes later and said, "Okay, they're going to fit us in at one. It'll take us a good forty-five minutes to get to town, so we should leave at noon. Then I have to meet a man about some cattle." He started rummaging through the box, shoving his hand in and lifting papers out.

Laura was still stuck on cows. What the heck was he talking about? "Andy, why are you talking to someone about cattle?"

He gave her a distracted glance. "Oh, I'm going to raise some. I'm thinking forty head to start."

She stared at his back. He was talking as if this was something they'd agreed on. The fact was that Laura didn't know the first thing about cows, except that they smelled and made a lot of noise. "Why cows, Andy?"

"What?" he said, as if he didn't understand.

Andy just did things, and as far as his work went—well, he was wealthy—or rather his family was. Laura had never really understood exactly what it was he did—aside from making deals, and investing and managing his wealth. There had always been a Great Wall between her and his work. She had never asked before, but now she felt she had to.

"Andy, I've always stayed out of your work, but I've got to ask: What are you doing, and why are you going into the cattle business? I think I should really know, as your wife, if there's going to be a herd of cows running around the property. You've always made these decisions for us ..." She stopped when he set down the papers and turned around to face her. For a moment, she wondered if he was about to dismiss her.

"You don't need to worry about money, Laura," he said. "I'll always have enough to provide for you and the kids. You won't want for anything."

"I know that, Andy, that's not what I'm saying. You've always looked after us. I wish you would share a little more with me. You don't share everything, Andy. You never have. With your work, you keep me out of it. I understand you just want to protect us, but by not talking to me about what you're doing, I feel as if there's a part of your life you're still keeping separate from me. Something I'm not a part of."

There, she had said it. She took a breath, feeling a type of confidence she had never felt before. She wondered what Andy was going to say. What would he do? He was an impossible man to read and when he gave her all of his attention, she felt special and loved. But at times like this, he had an unpredictable, predatory look that would have once made her back away—before she knew him. He dropped a folder and set his hand on his hip. Of course, her eyes went right there. The man was drop-dead gorgeous, sexy, and she remembered what it was like to have those hips settled against her.

"You're right. I'm sorry," he said.

Laura couldn't have been more shocked. Her jaw slackened as her brain scrambled to figure out what to say. She had expected him to do what he always had; tell her not to worry, that he'd take care of everything and she didn't need to know. *What the hell?*

"Oh, thank you," she said.

A hint of amusement brightened his eyes, and she knew he was taking some enjoyment from seeing her rattled and knowing he was responsible for it. He sifted through the rest of the box, one she recognized as being from his office. "Did you come across a big manila envelope with a small tape recorder in it? I swear it was in this box," he said, distracted again.

"No, I didn't. Is it important?" she asked. As far as bills, paper, and all that, Andy had always looked after everything.

He seemed to stiffen and kept sifting through the box. When he answered her this time, he didn't look at her. "Nothing for you to worry about," he said. "It's just something I need to keep track of."

Laura nodded, wondering at the steel wall that seemed to have come down around him. What was it about that envelope that was so important?

Chapter 7

Andy was sitting in one of the two chairs across from the doctor's desk, Gabriel tucked against him on his lap. The little boy, who worshipped Andy, snuggled against him as if he knew he alone would protect him and would never allow any harm to come his way—and he wouldn't, ever. He loved Gabriel like he loved his own children.

Andy was still bothered about that tape and the envelope. He was positive he had put it in the box with all his bank papers and investments, as he liked to keep everything together. He'd look again when he got home. That envelope was better than a smoking gun. It was his only protection from what his mother had done, trying to take the babies away and get rid of Laura. He still couldn't believe the threats his mother had made to set up Laura on some trumped-up crime. Getting her locked away just to be rid of her. His mother was powerful, coming from Eastern bluebloods and a long line of politicians-she was a snake. Andy planned to keep his family as far from her reach as possible. His father, well, who the hell knew where

Todd was. Probably off with one of his mistresses. Andy hadn't spoken to him since marrying Laura instead of a senator's daughter, as had been planned for him.

Andy glanced over at Laura. Her short hair had a little natural curl and she'd stuck a barrette in each side to hold it back, making her appear a very young twenty-one-year-old, even though she was far older in terms of what she had suffered and endured. She was so damn honest, kind, good and vulnerable. Whether she knew it or not, she did need protecting. The babies were both asleep in their carriers on the floor beside her, the bulky diaper bag at her feet. She smiled at him nervously, fiddling with her fingers and her ring.

She was on edge and had been throughout the exam. All the questions had fallen on her, but that was only after the doctor had asked how old she was. After that, the questions seemed beyond routine. Had she kept his vaccinations up to date? Did she feed him a balanced diet? How long had she ignored his fever and what had taken them so long to seek medical attention? Andy had been stumped for a second until he realized the doctor's stern line of questioning was more about her age—or so he thought, anyway. When Andy asked the doctor if that was the same line of questioning he used on every parent who walked through his door, the doctor had simply smiled and said it was routine.

To Andy, that response sounded evasive, but once Andy made it clear Laura was his wife, the doctor had seemed to read the writing on the wall. The change in his tone from questioning to respectful was alarming. Then again, this wasn't North Lakewood and people here didn't know the Friessen name. Andy was determined to earn a reputation in this community so that when people, like this doctor, spoke to Laura, they would do so with respect.

"Don't be so nervous," Andy finally said when Laura started biting the corners of her nails. He always knew when she was pulling away. Something was eating at her and she just didn't have the experience to know how to hide it from him. He supposed that was something that would come with age, but he hoped Laura would never learn to hide her feelings. Andy just didn't want that in a woman. He'd grown up with dishonest, polished, skilled women all around him and had realized he didn't like that one bit. It was refreshing to have a wife as naïve as Laura was.

"Did you hear the way he talked to me?" she said. "It's been a while since someone has talked down to me like that. I wonder whether he even realized you were there? It pissed me off, Andy, when you had to tell him I was your wife. What was that look you two exchanged?"

Yeah, she was more than rattled—she was upset. He didn't like seeing her this way, and he didn't like the expression the doctor had worn, as if Andy had robbed the cradle. "Just setting the record straight," Andy said. "He won't talk to you that way again. It was inappropriate—he knows it and I know it. He may not understand what it means to deal with a Friessen."

The door opened, and the doctor stepped in, wearing a dark sweater. He'd shed his white doctor's coat but still had a stethoscope draped around his neck. This time, when he took in Laura and then Andy, his expression changed to something that had Andy holding Gabriel a little tighter.

He sat at his desk, opened the file he was carrying and scribbled a few notes before setting down his pen and looking at them both. "The twins look great, if you could sign the transfer papers from your pediatrician in North Lakewood, I'll get the records up here," he began. "Jeremy appears bigger than his sister, which happens sometimes with twins. Both are right on track as far as growth and weight development, which is good. Now, I just wanted to ask, because I have both Chelsea and Jeremy as O negative blood types. Laura, you said you're O, and you too, Andy, but Gabriel is A negative, so …" He stopped talking, and Andy didn't miss what he was getting at. Laura obviously didn't either, as she'd already lowered her head as if she had something to be ashamed of. Andy wasn't just angry but pissed. It was as if this guy knew exactly which buttons to push with him.

"I'm not really sure what you're getting at here, and I really don't appreciate what you're insinuating or the way you keep talking to my wife," Andy snapped.

"What I'm getting at, is that you couldn't have fathered Gabriel. The father would need to be blood type A or B, and you are neither, as you said. How old are you, Laura?"

This was the first time Andy could remember feeling as if someone was judging him and Laura, questioning their business. What was this guy trying to do, asking Laura's age? Yeah, if he was Gabriel's father, it would have been statutory rape. He knew it, and obviously everyone here did, too, making it the elephant in the room.

"I'm Gabriel's father in every way that counts, so what is this really about?" Andy said. He glanced over at Laura's flushed face. He wasn't about to allow this prick into his private business—he was walking a fine line as it was.

The doctor gestured as if everything was cool, but he didn't even look Laura's way. "Well, for one, I need to have all the information. A complete history is essential for a proper diagnosis. How old were you when you had him?"

"I had just turned sixteen," Laura whispered, and Andy could hear her pride take a hit.

"What are you doing? What the hell does her being sixteen have to do with any of this?" Andy glanced down at Gabriel, who was cuddled against him. His eyes fluttered open and then closed again. Andy hoped he wasn't really listening to what was being said.

"I just want to get a picture of the situation," the doctor said.

"Picture of the situation? Sounds more like you're trying to stir up trouble."

The doctor set his pen down, and his leather chair whooshed as he leaned back. "Look, I just don't like parents hiding things. Before you get upset, I need to run more tests on Gabriel. From the blood we drew, the lab reported his white cell count is unusually high."

"What does that mean?" Andy asked. Laura's eyes widened, and she looked to him for help. He could tell the doctor had not only pushed all her buttons but also had her teetering on the edge of a breakdown.

"It means there could be some infection," the doctor said. "Until I get all the tests back, I won't know for sure. I don't like to just hand out prescriptions for antibiotics. If there's an infection, I want to know why and what's causing it—whether it's viral or bacterial. If it's more serious, I also need the father's medical history as well. That's why I asked, because neither of you shared the fact that Gabriel is not Andy's biological child." He looked at each of them in turn.

Andy hadn't thought too much about the boy who had fathered Gabriel, and as Gabriel snuggled in closer and gripped his shirt, he liked it even less that Gabriel wasn't his. "He's not in the picture, so what about in the meantime?" Andy asked.

The doctor slid the paperwork across the desk. His expression was concerned enough that Andy felt all kinds of alarm bells going off. "Well, until I get Gabriel's records, I need to know from you what has been prescribed in the past. Would you be able to find out the father's medical history?"

He looked to Andy for the answers, even though he had only come into the picture a year ago, when Gabriel was four. Andy had never spoken to Laura about the father. All he knew was that the boy had wanted nothing to do with Laura after finding out she was pregnant, and that her parents had asked her to leave. Maybe Andy had left her past alone for too long. He was pretty sure Gabriel had missed out on medical care and dental appointments. Andy had just assumed everything had been taken care of, but Laura wouldn't have had any health insurance. She and Gabriel had barely been getting by.

"I don't think he's ever taken anything, has he, Laura?" Andy said. He hadn't meant to put her on the spot, but Laura just shook her head. He didn't miss the shadow that fell over her as she slouched a bit, trying to hide. She swallowed and looked to Andy, and now she was wringing her hands. Andy wondered what that was about. What he did know, was that he and Laura needed to sit down and have a heart-to-heart. Maybe it was time he found out everything that had happened to his wife and Gabriel before he knew them, before she ended up a maid in the Friessen mansion.

Andy reached for the orders for blood work, glancing at all the boxes checked off. It was a lot of tests for his little boy and Andy worried now about whether it was even the flu.

"Oh, I put a rush on the tests. If you could go downstairs to the lab right now, they'll have the results back to me today," the doctor said. He closed up the file and scooted back his chair, giving them a practiced smile before he left.

Chapter 8

"I know we've never talked about it Laura, and I didn't ask, because it didn't matter-but I'm asking now. I need you to tell me everything," Andy said. He crossed his arms and leaned against the counter, looking down at Laura as she scrubbed the skillet she had used to brown the chicken before setting it in the oven. She scrubbed vigorously over a spot he could see was already clean. He could tell by how hard she went at it that she didn't want to talk about a past that he knew was painful, though it had shaped her into who she was today.

"Hey." He set his hand on her shoulder and rubbed until she looked up at him, he could see just how much she still hurt over those lost teenage years.

She blinked for a second, fighting against the memory. When she opened her amazing green eyes, even the gold flecks that always sparkled with life had dimmed with sadness. "I never took Gabriel to the doctor before because I couldn't afford it. There was a free clinic on Fridays, but I could never get there because I had to work. He never got sick anyway. He had the odd cold or sore throat, but he was fine. Am I a bad mother?"

"No, of course not. I know how you struggled. I saw what you had to live in. You did the best you could."

Laura set her hands on the rim of the sink and stared out the window. "I don't know, Andy. I wondered, at times, if I was selfish for not giving him up, but I couldn't. He was mine. I love him."

"Hey, that's not selfish. None of that matters now, anyway. If you hadn't made the choices you made, I wouldn't have met you and Gabriel," he said. That got a smile out of her.

"Yeah." She tapped the sink with her fingers.

"I know your parents asked you to leave when they found out you were pregnant, and that the boy who knocked you up wasn't involved. Did he even meet Gabriel? Tell me everything," he said. He waited for her to respond, watching as she squeezed her hands, touching the wedding ring he'd set on her finger, turning it around and around. He knew it meant something to her—meant everything to her.

"Dad was an elder in our church, one of the youngest, and Mom was so proud. Her father was a Lutheran minister, so we had a strict household, you could say. We were raised in the church in Arlington, an Anglican Church called The First Savior. We attended every Sunday. I even helped run the Sunday school when I was fifteen, with my mom." She sighed. "You know, today, at the doctor's office, I realized you've moved us right back into the Bible Belt. I swear Andy, I will never set foot back in a church, but here we are. I may be young, but I know communities where the church is the hub. I know how people respond to us 'sinners.'"

"I think you're reading too much into it. That doctor could just be a prick, is all." Andy had never considered religion when he bought the house, even though he was aware that some counties and communities were run by their churches. It was something he had heard in passing, but he had never given it much thought. He wondered, could she be right?

"I first met Tyler at church, when his family moved nearby. I was twelve and he was a year older than me. We also went to the same school. His sister, Melinda, and I were friends. We were all part of the youth group at our church."

Laura was still gripping her wedding band and she wouldn't look up at him. Andy wasn't religious. With his family, walking into a church was all about politics, who you knew, and what you were trying to get. It was about keeping up appearances.

"We were only together once, Andy. It was on a school ski trip. He snuck me into his room when everyone was on the hill. I didn't enjoy it, it hurt and we used no protection. I didn't plan it. I got pregnant. I knew something was wrong, because I didn't feel well and had missed my period. Mom took me to my family doctor, who told me I had to tell my parents, because otherwise he would. That was the first time I lied to Mom, said the checkup was fine. I couldn't tell her then. I tried to tell Tyler first-but ever since …"

She was having trouble finishing, and Andy had a pretty good idea about what had happened. The kid was all about sex. He had screwed her, so he was done with her and had moved on to the next girl. Her eyes were streaked with tiny red lines as she fought to hold on to all her sorrow and heartache.

"He avoided me after we had sex. I think he was disappointed, because it got awkward and weird. Anyway, I cried for days and Mom kept asking what was wrong. I didn't want to tell her, but I was running out of time. My waistline was starting to disappear and I knew I wouldn't be able to hide it much longer with the clothes I had. I was four months pregnant. Mom noticed and started asking me why I was gaining weight. I knew I had to say something, so I waited until after church one Sunday, after our Sunday dinner, and then I asked Mom and Dad if I could talk to them. Maybe I thought they'd be more forgiving of me, it being Sunday. When I told them, Mom started crying and then yelled at me. She called me a slut and slapped me across the face. Dad … I'd never seen him look at me with such disappointment before.

"They made me feel ashamed and dirty and I wanted to crawl into a hole and die. I had never imagined it could get much worse, but I was so wrong. It was awful. They sent me to my room and then forbade me from going to school the next day. My two younger brothers—Chad was eight and Brian was twelve—knew something was wrong and they kept asking why Mom and Dad were so upset. They thought I had been kicked out of school and they asked me what I'd done, but I couldn't tell them. When they were at school the next day, Dad came home early and he and Mom sat at the kitchen table, side by side, holding hands, looking across at me as if I was a stranger. I felt so alone.

"It was Mom who said I had to get rid of it. I was shocked she would even say it, as the church is so against abortion. I couldn't do it, Andy. No matter how terrified I was, there was a life growing inside me and I couldn't abort him. I said no. I don't know where I found the courage to stand up to her. Mom handed me a suitcase and said I had to leave. She wouldn't allow me to remain under their roof as a bad influence on my brothers, putting a blemish on the values they had tried to instill in us. I was fifteen and terrified, a disappointment to my family. Dad didn't say a word. He wouldn't even look at me as he got up and walked away. It was horrible. I begged Mom. I even got down on my knees. I was crying, and she just shook her head and told me to leave. So I packed the suitcase and walked out the front door. I was humiliated-the neighbors were outside, watching. I'm sure they'd heard the yelling.

"I just started walking. I went to Tyler's house and waited around the corner until I saw his car pull into the driveway. I thought for sure he'd at least help me—after all, it was his child. When he opened the door and saw me standing there, with a suitcase, he got worried. At first I thought it was for me, but I quickly realized when I heard a girl inside that he was worried for himself. I told him I was pregnant, that he was the father and that my parents had thrown me out. He just told me to go away and he shut the door in my face. I never saw him again-and I never saw my parents, either."

She dipped her hands in the water, and Andy could see her shaking. He stepped behind her and slid his arms around her, holding her tight. He rested his cheek against her head.

"I'm so sorry, Laura," he said. He wanted to kill her parents. He wanted to seriously hurt them—and Tyler, too.

She nodded, choking back a sob. "You know, it was so hard, Andy. I was terrified. I walked for hours and I didn't know where to go or who to call. I went to a shelter, and they asked me how old I was. So I lied. I said I was sixteen because I was afraid someone would try to take my baby from me or force me to get an abortion. I got a job at a fast food restaurant, but I started to show-and the social workers came sniffing around. They asked me who my parents were, how old I was, telling me I had a future ahead of me and was too young to raise a child. They kept asking what I was going to do with the baby.

"When I went into labor, I took a cab to the hospital. Someone there called the social worker, who showed up when I was in labor. I thought they were going to take Gabriel from me. I called my mom and she said I could come home if I gave up the baby. She said everything would go back to normal. I hung up that payphone and left the hospital with Gabriel. We left Arlington and that was how we ended up in North Lakewood. I met Aida, and she got me the job at your parents' mansion."

Andy just held her. He had heard the last part of her story from Aida, and he knew it was worse than she was saying. He couldn't imagine how tough it had been for her to feed Gabriel, let alone herself. She had been forced to work and find someone else to look after her son. Andy lowered his head as he remembered Aida, that sweet old woman, who had put up with no crap from him and had called him out on every dumb-ass thing he'd done. Aida had killed herself and left him a tape recording so he'd know just how horrible his mother was. Caroline Friessen had discovered Aida's past. The fact that she'd been in prison and had jumped parole. Caroline was blackmailing the old woman to secure her help in getting rid of Laura. In the end, Aida hadn't been able to live with the threat and she had taken her life instead—leaving the evidence for Andy. He still didn't know what he'd do with it. If

Laura knew the truth, if she found out that Aida hadn't simply died in her sleep, it would destroy her.

"It's okay. You know I'm never going to let anyone hurt you and Gabriel, or our babies," he said.

She nodded again, turning in his arms and pressing her face against his chest. "I love you so much, Andy," she said. He held her as he whispered, "I love you, too."

Chapter 9

"Andy, can you grab the phone while I get dinner on the table?" Laura called out. The babies were in their swing, going back and forth and Gabriel was propped up on the sofa. The TV was on and he was watching *Spiderman*. Laura wondered whether he was actually watching, considering he kept closing his eyes and nodding off. She set her hand on his forehead, and he barely responded. "Are you feeling any better?" she asked. "Do you think you can eat some dinner?"

"No," he grumbled in a sleepy voice.

When Laura looked up, Andy was standing in the archway between the kitchen and living room, wiping his scruffy face with his hand. His expression was grim and he was still holding the phone when he gestured her over.

"Andy, what's wrong?" she asked.

He set his hand on her shoulder and guided her just inside the kitchen. "That was the doctor. Gabriel's white blood cell count is too high—we have to bring him in to the hospital now," Andy said. He had to clear his throat. "Laura, he has leukemia."

Laura couldn't form a thought. She felt the floor soften beneath her even though she was standing there with Andy. She felt cold and numb. For a moment, all she could do was breathe. She couldn't understand what he was saying. Maybe he realized that was exactly what was happening, as he set his hand on her shoulder and squeezed, leaning in and really looking at her. She could see the glassy look in his eyes, as if he was fighting back tears, and she knew it was bad. She threw her arms around his neck and just held on. "Andy …" She choked as a tear slipped down her cheek, then another and another. She didn't let go of him.

She could feel him tighten his hold on her, rubbing her back as he breathed her in. "We have to go now, Laura. The doctor's going to meet us at the hospital."

She was shaking when she pulled away. She glanced at the chicken she'd just taken out of the oven and set on the table. It was only a momentary thought; dinner was ready, they couldn't go yet. It was so surreal. Suddenly, she was with Andy, bundling up the twins and going out the door and into the truck. Andy simply scooped up Gabriel and buckled him in the back with the twins. Gabriel continued to sleep as they drove to Columbia Falls—to the new children's hospital.

Doctor Bruce Siegel had been waiting for them when Andy carried Gabriel in. Laura followed with both babies in their carrier, side by side. Gabriel was settled into a bed in a private room and a nurse helped him into a hospital gown. A hospital ID bracelet was fastened to his wrist. Laura just watched helplessly while Gabriel cried as he was stuck with a needle and an IV was threaded into the back of his hand; Andy stepped in and talked him through it. Laura was still reeling, trying to wrap her head around the fact that her little boy didn't just have the flu. They'd just moved to another state, they hadn't even unpacked the boxes and her son was now in a hospital bed—and Andy was the one trying to calm him down.

Jeremy started fussing, and Laura stuck a soother in his mouth and lifted him from the carrier. Andy glanced over and must have seen her struggling—he stepped closer and took Jeremy from her arms. As soon as he did so, Chelsea decided to fuss.

"Can I speak with you two outside?" the doctor said, gesturing to the door. Laura and Andy stepped out into the hallway, each holding a baby. The hallway was busy with nurses and orderlies going back and forth while families waited. "Andy, as I said to you on the phone, what I suspected was leukemia has actually come back as AML, acute myeloid leukemia, which is very aggressive."

Laura looked to Andy. She'd never heard of this before.

"How aggressive are you talking? You have treatment, right? I know leukemia is curable," Andy said. He was using that all-business tone and he expected answers. Laura was glad he was talking because she didn't understand and her mind couldn't formulate any rational questions—unlike Andy. Treatment had come a long way over the years, that much she did know.

"With the type your son has, we need to start an aggressive round of chemotherapy to kill all the cancer cells in the blood and bone marrow, which will put the cancer in remission. After the chemotherapy, we'll need to perform a stem cell transplant. We don't want the leukemia cells to spread to the brain or the spinal cord, and we still need to run more tests to make sure it hasn't. Once we know what stage he's in, we'll begin treatment, possibly in rounds, but a lot depends on what these next tests show."

Laura could hear Gabriel crying behind her, and Chelsea, who was rubbing her eyes, was starting to fuss again. Her baby wanted a stress-free mama, but what she was getting was a mother wound so tightly she was barely holding it together. "So let me understand this: You're going to start this treatment right now, and then what?" Laura asked. She knew she had to sound frantic.

"Yes, but first we have more tests to do, and then his treatment team, the Oncologist and the social worker, will assemble. We need to find out how advanced the cancer is, then we'll have a better idea of the outcome from there."

Laura was still stuck on the words "social worker." *What the fuck?* She'd lived this nightmare once before. Andy must have been wondering the same thing, as he shook his head and added: "What exactly is the role of the social worker? Last I heard, they don't have medical degrees and have no business getting into my son's care."

"It's nothing like that. I don't know what you're worried about, but a social worker is always provided for families to help with the emotional and physical aspects of treatment. They're there to help you find services you may need," Doctor Siegel said.

Laura wasn't sure she felt any better. The doctor still sounded like he was pushing some agenda. Maybe she was being unreasonable, but it still felt as if people were sticking their noses into her family's business.

"Any services we need, I'll find them," Andy snapped, and Laura was glad he had.

"That's your choice," Siegel said. "The social worker is only there to make it easier for you and your family. Now, I wanted to talk to you about a donor for the stem cells. There's a donor bank, but a family match is ideal. Andy, you're not the father, but you can still be tested. We're not looking to match blood type but rather six key antigens. The best match is always a family member."

"You can test me," Laura said.

"Of course. We also need to look for donors, which takes time, and we need to have the donor ready by the time the chemo has killed all the leukemia cells." The doctor checked his watch. "Okay, I have to make rounds, but we need to do a lumbar puncture tonight. We'll sedate Gabriel, but one of you should be here. One of the interns will be by to get you set up for your tests." The doctor patted Andy's shoulder and glanced Laura's way, then he left.

Laura couldn't think of one intelligent thing to say or do. She just stood there, waiting for someone to say something, anything.

"Laura," Andy said.

She started and looked up at him. "Yeah, what are we going to do?"

"I'm going to stay tonight. You're going home with the babies, and——"

"No," Laura said, cutting him off. There was no way she was leaving her little boy. She was almost frantic when Andy grabbed her shoulder and gave a little shake.

"Hey, stop it. Listen, you go home. We can't both stay tonight, not with the babies, and you're still nursing. It's just for tonight, Laura. Take the truck. I'll call you later, after they do the tests …"

"Excuse me," a young man in blue scrubs interrupted. "Doctor Siegel said you were going to be tested as a match for your son." He looked to Laura and then Andy. "We can do it right now, all of you. Doctor Siegel asked for a rush."

"You go first," Andy said, "and then you take the babies home."

Gabriel cried out again and Laura started into his room when Andy touched her shoulder to stop her.

"I'll stay with Gabriel," he said. "It's important you be tested right now. You'll be the closest match as his mother."

When Laura looked up at Andy, her strong, sexy alpha male who could handle anything, she could see the tension and worry he was doing his very best to hide. He was her super hero, her knight in shining armor and she wondered if he would ever ask for help.

Chapter 10

It was horrible, the way Gabriel cried when they stuck him with a needle again to sedate him. Andy knew his son was terrified, so he snapped at the nurse or the intern or whoever it was to give them a minute. Maybe that was why the doctor was called in.

"Andy, you have a second?" Doctor Siegel asked after Gabriel was quiet and sleepy, which took less than a minute after the sedative had been given.

Andy wanted to pull his hair out, he was so frustrated. He wanted Gabriel to be all right so he could take him home. He couldn't believe this was happening. They were all healthy, every one of them, or they should have been. Andy had the money and resources to make sure of it, but the cancer inside the little boy, who was his in every sense except biologically…he couldn't make that go away, and it left him feeling powerless.

He didn't say anything as he followed the doctor into the hallway, his shoes squeaking on the polished floor. The doctor had changed into blue scrubs, and he appeared even younger than when they had first met, maybe in his early forties.

"I wanted to talk to you about your wife," the doctor said.

Andy stiffened and had to fight the urge to roll his shoulders back and keep his hands relaxed. He was ready to put his fist through a wall if it would get him somewhere, anywhere, because he wasn't going to let anyone put his wife down or criticize her.

"She's not a match and you are a long shot," Siegel said. We'll look for an unrelated donor, but that can lead to complications. I need to stress that time is not on our side, and depending on the outcome of the test tonight …"

"Stop," Andy interrupted. He needed to get a grip, as he was misreading everything. "Explain in English, please. What are you looking for? What do I need to do? My wife isn't here, so I don't want you to hold anything back. Where are we, exactly?"

The doctor's expression turned grim. "Exactly? Well, not good. From the preliminary blood work that came back, I'm concerned about how far the cancer has already spread. The lumbar puncture for the spinal fluid and the bone marrow aspiration and biopsy will tell us a lot more, but this type of leukemia is aggressive and will spread to the brain, spleen, spinal cord, liver and lymph nodes. Right now, I don't know the stage, so we need to find him a match quickly. The tissue type has to be identical to Gabriel's, and that means a family match is what we need. You have to uncover every family member related to Gabriel and get them in here to be tested. Again, the outcome of the tests tonight will decide the course of the chemotherapy and possibly radiation, including how radical we need to be. We're destroying all the cancer cells in the marrow along with all the healthy ones, meaning his immune system will be damaged. Do you understand what I'm saying?"

Andy didn't need a medical degree to know how serious the situation was. "We need that match as soon as you finish the cancer drugs, or my kid's dead. Does that sum it up?" he said. His chest squeezed with a pain he wished could be physical, because this was beyond anything he'd ever experienced.

The doctor shoved his hands in his white coat pockets and squared his shoulders. "Yes."

"So I need to find someone from Laura's family or the family of the kid who fathered Gabriel, and hopefully one of them will be a match, right?"

"The more family members you can find so we can test them, the better chance we have of finding a match. Depending on the outcome of the biopsy, we have a week or two at the most."

It was worse than Andy thought. He rubbed his scruffy jaw, and the doctor was pulled away by a nurse only to return a few minutes later.

"Okay, we're going to take him up now," Siegel said. "We'll get you gowned up so you can come in with him, and you can see him right after the procedure."

Then the doctor was gone, and Andy stepped back into his little boy's hospital room. For the first time ever, he wondered what the hell he was going to do.

Chapter 11

It wasn't often that Laura drove, and she could count on one hand the number of times she'd driven Andy's fancy truck. He would never let her drive him around, not in this lifetime. He'd once said to her that men drive women, not the other way around. Laura understood that was just the way Andy was. He took charge, made the decisions and protected her and her children. He just had a very strong opinion of what real men were, but then, all the Friessen men were like that. Meeting his cousins, Jed, Brad and Neil, Laura had seen it firsthand.

She had also seen what it was to be loved by a Friessen man. It was a powerful and overwhelming feeling that she'd had to get her head around quickly, or else she was positive she would have lost her sense of self. She remembered how Andy had barked out that there was no way in hell she would drive while he sat idly on the passenger side like some useless namby-pamby—those had been his exact words. There was something about that memory that eased the overwhelming despair she felt now. Her husband saw the roles of men and women as being so very black and white.

The headlights on the truck flashed over another pickup when Laura pulled up to the front of the house. When she turned off the truck and slid out, she saw Kim stepping out of her own truck and coming around the back end. She wore a heavy coat and blue jeans, her hair in a ponytail.

"Hey there, Laura," Kim said. "Hope you don't mind me just showing up here, but your husband called from the hospital and asked if I'd check on his horse, feed her and give you a hand if you need it. He sounded worried on the phone."

Laura put her hand on the back door and wondered if Kim had picked up on her annoyance. She hated when Andy did this. It made her feel useless, as if he didn't trust her. After all they'd been through together, she hoped he'd be past pulling stunts like this. "We're fine," Laura said, though she knew they weren't. She ached and worried, and she knew she wouldn't get a wink of sleep tonight. She was just being stubborn, digging her heels in to make a point, and she grumbled to herself.

"I wouldn't be, Laura," Kim said. "I'd be a basket case if it was my kid in the hospital and I was sent home with the babies. I can only imagine how helpless you feel."

Laura's eyes burned, and she fought back the tears. Maybe Kim really did understand. Maybe she should stop being such a cranky-pants.

Kim reached over and rubbed her shoulder. "Hey, you're not alone. Why don't I help you in with these babies, make us some coffee or something, and you tell me when to go home? Around these parts, we tend to look after each other," Kim said in a kind and supportive way that took the edge off Laura's irritation.

Laura didn't say anything for the longest time, as she didn't like asking for help from anyone. Andy knew that. Maybe that was why he had phoned Kim. She was still irritated, because it felt as if he had done it behind her back, but she said, "Okay, sure."

Kim helped her inside with the babies. As Laura nursed, changed and bathed them, she could hear her neighbor in the kitchen, dishes clattering, most likely cleaning up the mess of their untouched dinner.

With both babies tucked in and asleep, Laura walked with unease down her hallway, taking in the open concept and all the wood. She hesitated in the doorway to the kitchen, watching Kim, who was humming away and looked so pretty in a light blue shirt. She had a trim figure, with curves in all the right places. She was taller than Laura, older and more confident. Laura wondered why Andy would call her. It bothered her immensely.

Kim glanced up. Her amazing deep blue eyes were filled with concern, which helped ease some of Laura's anxiety. She kept jumping back and forth like a seesaw with this ridiculous jealousy, reading something into it, that probably wasn't even there.

"I hope you don't mind, but I cleaned up a bit," Kim said. "Your dinner was out on the table, so I wrapped it up and put it in the fridge. It should still be good." She gripped the washcloth in her hands and looked suddenly awkward. "I hope I'm not overstepping, here. If I am, let me know. When your husband called and asked me to come over and help, I could hear in his voice how worried he was about you."

"Well, my husband shouldn't be calling other women to help me," Laura said. The minute she did, she wanted to take it back. She felt her face warm. "Sorry, that was …" She wanted to say "inappropriate."

Kim shook her head and stepped around the counter. "I understand how you feel, Laura. I did feel a bit awkward when your husband phoned, but any man who loves his wife as much as yours does, well … let's just say you're lucky to have a man who loves you so much that he doesn't leave you to figure out everything yourself. I can also see how you would find it irritating at times, though."

Kim had surprised her. Laura found herself wanting to confide just how frustrating it was at times, but she had to remind herself that she couldn't change Andy. He was an amazing man—except for the fact that he made her so mad at times like these.

"I'm sorry about Gabriel," Kim said. "Andy mentioned what they found."

Laura had to blink back tears as she struggled to hold it together. She'd been numb from the news and had wanted a moment to sit by herself and just cry; but she hadn't had a spare second to herself. Maybe that was why a tear leaked out before she could blink it back.

"Hey, listen, come and sit down," Kim said, rubbing her back and leading her over to a seat at the round oak table. Kim pulled a chair out beside her, and Laura tried to pull herself together. She nearly jumped when she heard the kettle shriek.

"I boiled water, thought you might like some tea. I was going to ask, if I could heat you up some dinner. Have you eaten?" Kim slid back the chair and unplugged the kettle.

"I'm not hungry, but tea would be nice," Laura said. "I know Andy did the shopping. Not sure what he bought, but check the cupboard by the sink. That's where the coffee and tea are."

Kim searched through the cupboard and pulled out a box. "Green tea," she said, holding it up.

"Sure," Laura said. She was about to say more but was

at a loss for anything else to talk about.

"I understand if you're not hungry, but you should try to eat something for those babies, at least. They need their mama healthy. I make a great omelette. Could I whip one up for you?" Kim offered as she made herself at home in Laura's kitchen, setting two steaming mugs on the table.

"You don't have to wait on me, Kim," Laura said. She glanced up at her neighbor, who was just trying to help and saw the awkwardness there. "Why don't I just drink this tea, and I'll think about the omelette?"

Kim winked at Laura. "Sure," she said, taking a seat across from her and setting her hands around her mug.

"Andy's supposed to call and let me know how Gabriel is...how the tests go," Laura said. "The doctor is running more tests tonight. I just don't know how this happened. I mean, before I met Andy, I really tried to make sure Gabriel was always healthy. I can't help thinking this is because of something I did."

Kim appeared confused for a second before she asked, "Gabriel isn't Andy's son?"

Why was Laura talking about this? The last thing she wanted was for more gossip to spread about her, for people to start talking about her misguided teenage years. She could feel her face burning. "No. Andy married me over a year ago, but he loves Gabriel as his own."

Kim reached forward and touched Laura's hands that were gripped together on the table. "That must have been hard for you before. You're so young. Is Gabriel's father in the picture?"

"No, Andy is Gabriel's father in every way that counts," Laura said. She wanted Kim to stop asking so many questions, but then, she needed to shut her own mouth and stop talking. She was only stirring the other woman's curiosity every time she spoke.

"I can tell," Kim said. "Any man that would accept a child as his own, the way your husband has, is worth keeping. You're lucky, Laura. I wasn't as fortunate." She glanced away, holding on to something that obviously bothered her a great deal.

"Are you married?" Laura asked. The fact was that she didn't know the first thing about Kim other than that she was their closest neighbor—and Andy, her husband, felt comfortable enough calling her.

"Once upon a time," Kim said. "I was very young and very stupid. I married the first young man to give me a lick of attention. It never would have worked. I was too immature, and he was too much a child himself. I grew up fast, though, and learned to stand on my own two feet. It was either swim or drown, and I learned a lot of things the hard way. At one time, I would have given anything to have a man as supportive as yours."

Laura wondered if she had pulled a face or something, because hearing that from Kim had her feeling threatened. Maybe she was setting her sights on Andy? Her rational mind said that was nonsense, but her self-conscious, irrational mind was running wild. Kim was confident, very pretty and closer to Andy's age. Why wouldn't he want her?

"I didn't mean to give you the impression I was after Andy," Kim said. "A man like him would never work for me now. I'm too … well, let's just say I do things my way, the way I want to do them, when I want to do them. I don't like answering to anyone. Besides, have you stopped and seen how that man watches you and cares for you? Anyone could see he's stuck his brand on you!" Kim laughed.

Laura had never seen her relationship with Andy that way. Sure, they'd worked through a lot, but he'd also only married her to protect her and Gabriel. She loved him deeply, so much that it hurt to breathe; and she knew he loved Gabriel as his own son.

Kim reached over and covered her hand. "Whatever you need, you just ask me. I'll stay all night if you need me. Don't feel threatened by me, Laura. Everyone needs someone, and I think we could be really good friends."

"Can I ask you something?"

"Sure, of course," Kim said before taking a swallow of her tea.

"That doctor you gave Andy the name of, is he any good?" Laura asked. She was still shaken by what an arrogant jerk he had been, in her opinion. He had judged her. She'd seen the way he looked at her, and could feel the disapproval in the way he'd talked to her. She should have been happy Andy had recognized that, but she wasn't.

"Bruce? Yeah, he's one of the best in this part of the country. I know he was offered a big opportunity in South Africa a few years ago but chose to stay. He's a great guy, and Gabriel couldn't be in better hands." She frowned. "Is there something wrong? It seems that wasn't the answer you were looking for."

"He said some things. I don't think he approves of me."

Kim appeared puzzled for a moment. "Really? That surprises me. I've known him a while from our church, and I haven't seen that in him. He's always so pleasant. Maybe you misread him. I mean, this is a stressful situation."

"Oh, I doubt that," Laura said.

Kim gave her another odd look and then appeared to consider something, but before she could say anything, the phone rang. Laura jumped up and raced for it, grabbing it before it could ring a second time.

"Hello?" she said, glancing over her shoulder at Kim.

"Hey, listen. Gabriel just finished with his tests. They

just moved him back to his room." Andy became quiet on the other end, and Laura's heart started pounding as her anxiety wound up. She wanted to scream. She felt absolutely helpless, being stuck at home instead of with her son.

"Andy, how is he?" She shoved her fingers through her hair, rubbing and pulling at a few knots.

"He's, uh … Laura, it's hard on him. I don't like seeing him like this. He's still asleep, but I'll be here when he wakes up."

Laura could feel her eyes burning as she listened to her husband. She willed her little boy to be okay, and she wanted more than anything to be there. For the first time in her life, she felt torn, as if caring for her babies was an obligation-and she couldn't shake her guilt at that thought. "What did the doctor say? What about the test?" she asked. She could hear the hesitation in Andy's voice and knew he was holding something back. That was what he did. He protected her, all of them, but this time she needed to know. "Please, Andy, stop hiding things from me. I really need to know. I want to come back there."

"You can't, Laura, not with the babies. They're still nursing. I wish a lot of things, honey, but I need you to be strong and I need you to get some sleep."

She could hear him sigh, and she pulled the phone away and shook her head. She wanted to yell at him, to reach through the phone and shake his arm, but she couldn't. He always had a way of holding back. "Please, Andy, don't hide anything. I know you're always trying to protect me, to protect us, but this is Gabriel—my little boy …"

"He's ours, Laura," Andy said, cutting her off, and she could hear in the sharp tone how thoughtless a remark that had been.

"You know that's not what I meant. I know you love

him, and he loves you so much," she said.

"Listen, I'll tell you more about what the doctor said tomorrow. The tests haven't come back yet, and we won't know anything about how far advanced the leukemia is or where they'll start his treatment until then," he said. "Are the babies asleep?"

"Yes. I'll come to the hospital first thing in the morning when they wake up. Oh, and Kim's here. You called her?" Laura mentioned. She glanced over her shoulder and noticed that Kim had picked up on the tension in the one-sided conversation.

"Yeah, I did. Laura, I didn't want you going home and being alone. I can't be there with you, so I'm glad she's there. Listen, go get some sleep, and I'll see you in the morning."

Laura held the disconnected phone and gazed out the darkened window. She heard a nickering and remembered Ladystar, Andy's horse. Kim must have heard, too, because she slid back her chair and said, "I'll go check on her again. I already filled her water and fed her."

"Thank you. I don't want to go and leave the babies alone in the house …"

Kim touched her arm. "Don't worry. I have a flashlight in the truck. I'll go take care of her. Did you want me to stay the night?" She slid on her coat.

Laura shook her head. "No, we'll be okay, but thank you for coming, even though it was my husband who asked you to."

"Don't mention it, Laura, and please call me, any time, day or night." Kim hesitated and then gave a sharp nod before stepping out the door. Laura slid the deadbolt home and listened to the truck door shut. She rested her head against the frame. Willing the morning to hurry and come, fearing this would be an awfully long night.

Chapter 12

Andy stared at the dark screen of his cell phone. Laura was at home with his babies, and the neighbor was there with her. Good. They were home, they were safe and at least he didn't have them to add to his worries. It wasn't that Laura worried him—she was one of the strongest, most amazing young women he'd ever met. She'd suffered and struggled for so long. He just couldn't bear to see the shadow of anxiety hanging over her. He'd never known what it was like to worry about putting food on the table, food in his mouth, a roof over his head or having to choose between going hungry or paying the heating bills. Laura had, and Andy had sworn she'd never have to live through that again. But this was her little boy. Gabriel, who had brought Andy and Laura together, was fighting for his life. For the first time in Andy's life, all his Friessen money meant nothing.

Starting out in Montana and moving his family here, was supposed to have been exciting. This was supposed to have meant a new life for them, a new place to watch his children grow up, a new place for them to live, to love and to laugh. When life decided to throw him a curveball, it hit like a five-ton steel shot, knocking him flat on his ass. The fact was, Laura had cornered him on the phone, and he didn't want to tell her what the doctor had said.

He hadn't even reconciled in his own mind what the hell they were going to do. He needed to think; to figure everything out and have some reasonable answers before he could tell Laura one word. The doctor had said that Gabriel had high-risk, abnormal mutations, which meant the cancer was aggressive and constantly changing. It had not only reached his blood, but was subtype M4, which the doctor had said was more likely to form masses. All Andy could make sense of was that this type of cancer was aggressive and moved fast. They needed a match, a family match—and now.

Andy walked over to the bed where Gabriel was fast asleep, tubes sticking out of his arm. He was so tiny, lying in that hospital bed. His dark, curly hair, a little too long, was stuck to the sides of his head. He was breathing evenly and deeply. Andy set his hand on his forehead and gently brushed the locks back. Gabriel stirred only to snuggle into Andy's hand, as if he knew he was there and his touch was all he needed. Andy could feel his eyes burning as he stared at this tiny bit of innocence, his little boy, who didn't deserve any of this. His nose was the same as Laura's, cute and pert, and he had her high cheekbones. Andy blinked and fought for a breath, trying to steady his nerves. He needed help. As he clutched his phone in his other hand, he considered what he had to do. He wasn't a match, and Laura wasn't close enough. God help him, but right now Andy was sure he'd bargain with the devil himself if that would save Gabriel's life.

He stepped away from the bed and dialed a number on his cell as he moved into the hall, walking past the open doorways in the pediatric ward. He listened to the ringing as he walked past each room, moms and dads and siblings with their sick kids, so many of them. He'd never for one moment realized how many children were suffering and fighting for their lives. It wasn't okay.

"Yeah?" a gruff voice barked over the line. Andy could hear from his cousin's voice that he'd been fast asleep.

"Neil, it's Andy. I know it's late. I'm sorry to wake you," Andy said. He wondered whether Neil could hear the shake in his voice, because this was the first time Andy had ever allowed such deep emotion to take him out at the knees.

"Andy, is everything okay?" Neil said. He must have picked up on something, as he sounded suddenly awake. Andy could hear his cousin's wife asking who it was, then Neil's muffled reply of "It's Andy. Go back to sleep" before he spoke again: "Andy, where are you? Have you settled into your new place? How did the move go?" There was rustling in the background as if Neil had climbed out of bed. Andy had to force himself to clear his throat so he could talk.

"We're in trouble. It's Gabriel. He's sick." It was all he managed to get out as he stood in front of the stairwell and then pushed the door open. He didn't want anyone to hear him, and the last thing Andy wanted to do was fall apart where someone could see. He stepped into the empty stairwell, letting the door swing shut behind him.

"Whoa, back up a second. What's going on?" Neil asked, sounding a bit frantic.

"Gabriel had a fever and we thought it was the flu, but he didn't get better, and we were getting worried. We took him to the doctor today. He has leukemia." Andy quickly shoved his fisted hand against his mouth as he felt himself choking up.

There was nothing but silence on the other end, and then Neil let out a sigh. "Oh my God, Andy. I'm so sorry. What did the doctor say? How bad is it?"

"It's leukemia, for fuck's sake, Neil. It's bad," he snapped, feeling bad the minute he did so. "I'm sorry."

"It's okay, Andy."

"I have to find him a bone marrow donor. He needs an ideal match, which is family. Laura's not close enough, and neither are the twins."

He could hear Neil groaning on the other end. "Andy, you can't do this alone. Do you want us to come? Candy and I'll get on a plane."

He swallowed for a second, because the fact was that he needed someone to watch his back. "Yeah, could you? I haven't told Laura how bad it is, and I'm worried. She's so tired now with the twins."

"Don't worry, we're coming. Candy and I'll help with the kids. Look, Andy, we'll help you figure this out. I'll call you when we land."

Andy felt such overwhelming relief as he stared at the disconnected phone. It should have been his parents he could call. Rallying them to his and Laura's side. At least he had his cousin Neil. Jed and Brad would come, too, if he called, but he stopped short of that. They would all come. They'd all stand with him, and they'd help him. He knew that. As Andy slumped to the concrete steps and lowered his face into his hands, he couldn't explain to anyone the sense of relief that filled him up. Neil was on his way. He'd never allowed himself to need anyone, to depend on anyone, until now.

Chapter 13

L aura stared at the clock beside the bed. The white glow of "5:59 AM" had burned into her eyes as she watched the time slowly tick by. Even though she was so tired that she couldn't sleep, she'd tossed and turned most of the night after feeding the babies and putting them back to sleep. When she crawled back into her own bed, she slid her hand to Andy's side, over his pillow, wishing he could be here so she could rest her head on his shoulder and feel his arms around her. Maybe her head, her mind, her thoughts could then stop racing to every nightmarish scenario she was trying to hide from.

She wondered if her sleepless night was just about her sweet little boy being so sick, or if it was also about her husband, who was the life force of their family. The man who held them together and took care of everything. She loved Andy so deeply. She just couldn't get her head around the fact that her little boy, whom she loved more than her next breath, was so gravely ill, and Andy was there with him. In that moment, she wished that Andy could be Gabriel's true, biological father. She wished a lot of things throughout the night. Crying into Andy's pillow until she had no more tears; beating herself up and letting herself wonder whether she was responsible for this. Maybe everyone had been right and she should have given Gabriel up when he was a baby, but she soon became angry at herself for thinking that way. How could she not, though? Until a year ago, she'd lived in nothing but dirty, unhealthy places because she couldn't afford anything else.

"Stop it," she muttered as she pressed her palms against her forehead and rubbed. She reached for the cell phone beside her on the nightstand, hoping Andy phoned in the night. She wanted to talk to him, to hear his voice. She only wondered for a second whether he was asleep as she pressed the number he'd programmed into her phone. That was just what he did. He set things up and organized them. Showing her only what he felt she should know. As she listened to the ringing, she knew Andy would censor any news.

"Hello?" He cleared his throat and sounded half asleep.

"Hi. I woke you." She sighed. Just hearing him breathe on the other end helped.

"Everything okay?" Of course, he was instantly alert.

"I couldn't sleep. Between worrying about Gabriel, and you not being here, it was a long night. How is Gabriel?" she asked.

"He's been asleep all night. You have to get some rest, Laura, or you're no good to the babies."

"I know Andy, but I can't rest here, when I'm worrying about what's going on there."

He sighed on the other end.

"As soon as the babies are awake, I'm coming in," Laura said. At the same time, she wondered how she could divide her time between her two babies and Gabriel. At times like this, she wished for family, for some support for her and Andy. Maybe she could talk him into calling his cousin Jed and his wife, Diana, who was Laura's friend and the closest person she had to family. Diana had always been there for her, even taking her in for a time.

"I called Neil," Andy said. "He's flying in with Candy to help. I know you want to be here, and …"

He stopped talking, and she realized then how tired he was. Whatever he was holding on to, he had almost let it slip. So there was more. She knew it deep inside of herself. She got out of bed and strode over to the window, shivering in the cold as she brushed back the curtain and stared out at the trace of snow on the ground just as the sun touched the horizon. She swallowed, irritated that Andy had called Neil without talking to her first. He had just made all the arrangements, which is what he did all of the time.

"It snowed last night, Andy. You could have mentioned you were calling your family," she snapped. The minute she said it, she wished she could take it back.

"Laura, you need some help—and I can only do so much. I need to be here, and it's best if Chelsea and Jeremy aren't here at the hospital, day in and day out."

"I know," she said. "I'm sorry. I'm just tired. I wish you'd talk to me more, tell me what you're thinking when you decide on something. I would kind of like to be consulted. Last night, you didn't tell me you'd called Kim. How do you think it made me feel, driving in here and finding her parked outside the house, hearing that my husband had called her. You made me feel incompetent."

"Laura, you're reading too much into it. I called Kim and my family for a lot of reasons. I didn't want you to have to struggle. I need to know you're okay. I feel helpless here with Gabriel; as if something has been taken from my control and I don't like it one bit. I'm sorry you felt slighted, but I'd do it again just to know someone was there for you."

He sounded irritated, and Laura felt bad. She knew this was the way he was. He was possessive, controlling, stubborn, strong and powerful. He'd seriously hurt anyone who tried to mess with them. She knew he loved them deeply, and to be truly loved by him, not just as an obligation, was a powerful thing that had her tearing up again.

"Andy, I love you, but you make me so frustrated when you won't talk to me about how you're feeling, about your decisions. I have a mind, Andy. I may be young, but I'm not helpless," she said. Jeremy picked that moment to cry out: "Jeremy's awake. I'm going to feed him, and as soon as they're both up, I'm coming in." She glimpsed Ladystar outside with her blanket on. "Andy, I forgot about Ladystar. I'll check on her and feed her before we go."

"No, you have enough to do with the babies. I'll call Kim, ask her to come by and feed the horse. Maybe I'll see if she can move Ladystar to her place. She has two Quarter Horses. You know what? I'll call Kim now and get her to drive you in. You've never driven on snow-covered roads. There could be icy patches out of nowhere. I don't want you taking any chances."

"No, Andy. You're not calling Kim to drive me. For the love of God, Andy—it's six in the morning! Like any sane person, she'll still be asleep. I can drive. I'll just be careful."

"No," he said. "I'll worry the entire way, and I have enough to worry about with Gabriel. I don't need to worry about you on the road. I'll grab a cab now, come home, shower, and change. I don't like leaving Gabriel."

"Andy, stop it! I'm not useless." Jeremy was getting louder as she started down the hall.

"Laura, that's not what I meant, and I don't want to

fight. I'm tired, and you're obviously taking this the wrong way. I'll just check with a nurse, and then I'll be on my way home."

He disconnected before she could say another word. She squeezed the phone, fighting the urge to toss it across the room. Instead, she tossed it on the rocker in the babies' room and lifted Jeremy from his crib. She wondered, as she strode back to her room to nurse Jeremy, when Andy would finally let her in.

Chapter 14

Of course, Andy walked in the door shortly after Laura had gotten dressed. This was the first morning she'd been alone in the house. Just her and the babies. Having no one to watch Chelsea and Jeremy while she showered had been nerve wracking. Andy stalked down the hall to their bedroom, boots scraping the hardwood floor, his hair unusually messy. The lines under his eyes showed how tired he was, but he was strong, too. He charged the air in the room every time he walked in. It became alive and powerful. That was what drew people to him. Laura figured he could command a battalion better than any general could.

"You ready?" he asked, taking in her wet hair, her bare feet and the turtleneck sweater she was still tucking into her jeans.

"Almost. I just have to change Chelsea and Jeremy and load up their diaper bag," she said, feeling a little awkward and hurt at the same time. "You know, Andy, I love you, but it hurts when you call another woman, even though you say it's to help me. I'm capable, yet you trust Kim more than me."

"Oh my God, Laura, would you drop this already?" His eyes flashed with anger as he snapped at her and continued into their bathroom.

"That's not fair, Andy. You're treating me like a child." She stood her ground, following him into the bathroom.

"Seriously, would you drop this? It's got nothing to do with me trusting Kim more than you. You're creating problems that aren't there. I called her because she doesn't have anyone, no husband, no kids and she's our neighbor. She offered, and you have your hands full. I'm not here to help you, Laura. I can't be in two places at the same time."

He yanked off his blue knit sweater, stalking out of the bathroom and tossing it on the unmade bed. Her eyes went right to his chest, that magnificent chest, and those strong, sculpted shoulders. He was absolutely ripped, and her body remembered what it felt like to be held against that chest, to rest her head on shoulders that were anything but soft. Being held by him made her feel as if she could take on the world. She loved to run her fingers through the dark hair covering his chest. She felt a lot of things when Andy was around, as he stirred passion, anger—every emotion inside of her. She'd give anything to have him with her. He sighed and shut his eyes. She knew he was coping with a lot. Maybe she was being unreasonable.

He started toward her, setting his hands on her shoulders. "Did you eat?"

Seeing the worry in his eyes, she felt like crap again, so she shook her head and touched his arm. A second later, she found herself pulled against his chest, breathing him in, loving the feel of him holding her.

"You have to eat. I'm not hungry, either, but we're not helping the kids if we don't eat. Go make us some eggs and coffee. I'll grab a shower, then we'll go." He rubbed her back as he spoke, and Laura didn't let go. She kept her arms where they were, around his waist. When Jeremy let out a squawk, she rubbed her face against his chest and rested her chin there, gazing up into his tired eyes.

"Your son is so demanding, just like his father," she said. She wondered if that amused him, but Andy had a way of thinking and holding on to things, making her wonder where his head was.

"And his sister is patient and quiet, just like her mama," he said. He slid his hand over her cheek and leaned down, pressing a light and tender kiss on her lips and just holding himself there. All the fire and love she felt, all of her need for him, seemed to grow in her heart, bigger and stronger than she'd ever thought possible.

He stepped away. "Go get our boy," he said. "I'll get in the shower."

Chapter 15

Laura had been especially quiet on the drive back to the hospital. Andy knew he'd made her angry, but he'd rather have her angry than stuck in the ditch, or hurt, or overwhelmed in any way. Maybe this was part of his desire to make things easier for her; to somehow make up for all her struggles as a teenage single mother, just trying to make ends meet. He knew she carried so much pain in her heart after what her parents had done—tossing her away instead of standing by her in her hour of need. When Kim pulled in right before they left, Andy had seen the way Laura frowned. She didn't pretend for a moment she was happy to see her. Kim, though, had been pleasant and neighborly. Andy had asked her if she could take Ladystar back to her place. Of course, she'd said yes. She was a nice woman, and he didn't understand why Laura didn't seem to like her.

As he glanced at his wife, quiet and staring straight ahead out of the windshield, he couldn't stay quiet. "You know, if you gave Kim a chance, Laura, she'd probably be a good friend to you. She didn't have to come over and help. She's being neighborly and kind and she's concerned about Gabriel," he said as he steered into the hospital parking lot and found a spot in the second row.

"Andy, I'm sorry if I seemed rude, but the fact that you called another woman … Kim is pretty, probably more capable than I am, closer to your age, smart and she would probably make your life easier. You just met her and you're already calling her," Laura snapped. She set her hand on the door handle to yank it open, but Andy reached over and grabbed her arm.

"Hey," he said. He had to fight the urge not to laugh. "Are you kidding me? You're jealous, that's what this is about? You think I would call another woman and have her show up to help you if I was interested in her?"

Laura gave him a look, her stunning green eyes flashing with what he was pretty sure was anger and hurt. He slid his hand behind her head and over her shoulder when she didn't answer him.

"I didn't notice whether she was pretty. I suppose she is if you say she is, but she doesn't interest me. You interest me. You're my wife. I just want you to be happy. I want to make things easier for you. Kim is our neighbor, and I just thought …"

"What did you think?" Laura snapped, her eyes now lit with a passion and fire that she couldn't hide. "Did you think I was so incompetent that maybe she could teach me something?"

Andy just watched her, trying to figure out how she could have taken the situation this way. He didn't pull his hand away as he glanced out the window, resting his other hand over the steering wheel. The irritation was coming off her in waves. She was even fisting her hands.

"Whatever she knows, whatever her experience is, I most certainly don't want you to ever learn from her. A woman like her, she's nice, but she has secrets and holds on to things. She has a past, and she doesn't interest me in the least. I don't want you ever learning how to hide something from me. Not ever, Laura," he said with a little more force than he'd meant. His point must have been clear to her, as her eyes widened and she started to speak before he interrupted. "You're the only woman who will be in my bed, under me. You're the only woman I'll bury myself in or whose lips will ever touch mine. So get it out of your head that Kim could interest me that way."

He was so close to her as he leaned down that her warm breath brushed his lips. She parted her lips slightly as she leaned in. He took what he felt was his, kissing her deeply until she was flushed and her every thought had disappeared.

"Are we clear now?" he asked.

She must have understood, as she licked her lips, breathing heavily. "Yes."

"Good. Now let's go see our kid."

He opened the door, got out and shut it a little harder than was necessary. All Laura had managed to do, was ramp up the fire between them. She was so inexperienced, that she had no idea of the depths of madness she could drive him to. He just prayed she'd never become an experienced woman, learning how to bring him to heel. He'd seen other women wrap their husbands around their fingers, but Andy swore no woman would ever do that to him. It struck him, as he reached Laura's side and opened her door, that her sweet smile touched his heart. Maybe it wasn't such a good idea to have Kim stopping over to visit his wife.

Chapter 16

Walking into Gabriel's hospital room and seeing her little boy so pale, lying there helplessly, made Laura feel like a horrible mother. She never should have made Andy feel he needed to leave her son alone just because she wouldn't call the neighbor. She knew deep down that she'd pushed every one of Andy's overprotective buttons. Her reasoning had been selfish. How could she have made him leave her son?

Andy carried both babies, a carrier in each hand, and set them on the floor in the room. Laura touched the rail and leaned over her son, smoothing back his bed hair, which was pasted to his forehead. The hospital blanket was tucked under his arms, and an IV tube was taped to the back of his hand. He moaned, and his eyes fluttered open.

"Mommy?" His voice was so weak, and she knew he had to be scared.

"I'm here. Did you have a good sleep?" Laura went to slide the side rail down so she could sit beside him on the bed.

"Don't do that, miss." A nurse hurried in around the other side of the bed. "We don't want him falling out accidentally."

"I'm his mother," Laura snapped. She was tired of people talking to her as if she didn't know any better. She continued to rattle the rail, trying to figure out how to move the damn thing, when Andy covered her hand with his and slid the rail down with a click. He set his hand on her back, standing beside her. The way he did it was so supportive, and just having him backing her up this way meant more to Laura than she could say.

He even set his one hand on her shoulder and the other on the bed beside Gabriel. "Hey, bud. Sorry I had to leave to get your mom and your brother and sister. Did you wake up when I was gone?"

"There were monsters," Gabriel cried. "I want to go home."

"It took us a while to calm him down when he woke up," the nurse said as she changed his IV bag and pulled a thermometer from her front pocket, setting it on the tray.

Laura slid her arms around him and tried to hold him, but he cried out. "I'm sorry, honey," she said. "Where does it hurt?"

"He'll still be sore where they did the puncture for the bone marrow," the nurse said as she took Gabriel's temperature. "Thatta boy, almost done."

"What puncture did they do?" Laura asked. She was reeling. She knew they had done tests, but she hadn't thought to ask the specifics. For some reason, she was thinking it would've been nothing invasive—maybe more blood tests or an x-ray, but a puncture?

"The bone marrow aspiration was taken from the hip, and he had a spinal tap," the nurse added. Laura's eyes widened as she glanced up at Andy. She should have been there.

"I was with him. I went in with him, Laura," Andy said, as if he knew where her thoughts had gone.

"The doctor will be in soon, and he wants to get started right away," the nurse said.

Laura wanted everyone to stop until she knew what the hell was going on with her little boy. She rubbed Gabriel's shoulder and his arm, wanting nothing more than to slip into bed with him, pull him into her arms and just hold him. He started fussing and tried to push the ear thermometer away.

"Hey, bud, it's going to be okay." Andy was rubbing Laura's arm and leaning down to Gabriel as if trying to hug them both. "Remember what I said to you last night, that I'm going to take care of everything?"

"I want to go home, Andy," Gabriel said. He was so scared, looking to Andy and then her. He loved Andy so much. He worshipped him, and she could see in his eyes how he truly believed Andy would take care of everything. The sun, the stars, the moon—everything set on Andy, and again Laura had to fight the urge to scoop her son up and run out of the hospital. She blinked back tears. Andy seemed to know she was struggling to hold it together, as he squeezed her shoulder. For a moment, it helped, and she took Gabriel's hand and just held it.

"Mommy is going to stay right here. The doctor is going to make you all better so you can come home."

"I want to go home now. Please, Mommy." He was going to start crying, and Laura knew they were coming to a point where he was going to be inconsolable.

"I'll be right back," the nurse said. Before slipping from the room, she turned and added, "You can hold him. Just be careful of his hip. It'll still be a little tender."

Andy went around to the other side of the bed, lowered the rail and slipped his hand under Gabriel's legs and shoulders, lifting him onto his lap. He glanced over at Laura. "It's going to be okay," he said. "Remember how I said there's a bug inside you, making you really sick? Well, that's why we're here. The doctor is going to give you some medicine that's going to kick this bug right out of you so you're all healthy and strong and …"

"And you're getting me a pony?" Gabriel asked weakly, though Laura picked up on the hope in his voice. Andy was nodding at her as he wrapped his arms around her son —their son.

"And you're coming with me to pick out your pony, and then you and I are going to herd some cattle," Andy said.

"Like real cowboys," Gabriel added as he fisted his tiny little hand in Andy's dark blue plaid shirt.

Andy rested his chin on top of Gabriel's head. "Yeah, like real cowboys, you and me."

Laura watched her husband and saw the love spilling over to her son. Her throat thickened and tears burned her eyes.

"Hey, you two."

Laura slid around at the familiar voice as Neil Friessen leaned down and took in the sleeping babies. He was Andy's very attractive, dark-haired cousin. He was well dressed, with the same height and build as Andy. He had the most charming smile, which lit up a room. His wife, Candy, was behind him, and she offered Laura a hesitant smile, her deep brown eyes and long, dark hair so distinct. She was beautiful and slim, and though she took in the room and the babies, she hung back. Anyone could read from her body language that she was uncomfortable.

"Neil, I thought you were going to call me when you got in?" Andy didn't move but kept Gabriel on his lap. The boy was more interested in staying right where he was, anyway—in Andy's arms.

Neil stood up and reached for Candy's hand, bringing her closer to the bed with him. They were both in blue jeans and light jackets. Neil had an energy about him that was so different from Andy's; he was vibrant and alive in a unique way. He drew people to him like a magnet. He knew just what to say and how to be with people to make them feel better, or so Laura remembered.

He touched her shoulder. "Hey, Laura, how are you doing?" he asked, watching her with such kindness.

She had to clear her throat before she could speak. "I'm good."

He exchanged a meaningful look with Andy and something passed between them privately. Of course, Laura couldn't help wondering what that was about.

A knock on the open door had them all looking at the light-haired doctor who'd set Laura's teeth on edge just the day before. He wore a white dress shirt and blue striped tie, with a white doctor's coat overtop. His hair was impeccable, and he looked to Andy first and then Neil, extending his hand. "I'm Gabriel's doctor, Bruce Siegel," he said. He gestured between Neil and Andy. "I can see the family resemblance. You must be brothers?"

"Cousins," Neil said, and the doctor nodded. He took in Laura and Candy and offered a polite smile. Neil moved back to allow the doctor to step by, but Laura had no intention of moving. Neil slid his arm around Candy's shoulders and pulled her closer.

"How are you this morning, Gabriel?" the doctor asked.

The little boy just shrugged and wouldn't let go of Andy.

"I know you're not feeling well, but we're going to give

you medicine that's going to help you get better," Doctor Siegel said. "We're going to get started this morning with the chemo. Hey, Gabriel, I want to talk with your mom and dad for a minute, and then I promise I'll give them right back."

Laura's head was reeling. So much had happened, so many decisions made, so many tests given without her consultation. First chemotherapy and then what treatment plan? They were starting now? She slid off the bed, her legs a little shaky.

Andy eased Gabriel back on the bed. He kissed him on the cheek and said, "I'll be right back. Don't go anywhere."

Laura touched her son and kissed him on the forehead. "You're going to be okay," she said. "I'll be right back."

Laura took in the babies, still sleeping, and then Andy came around the bed, holding his hand out to take hers. They followed the doctor to the doorway and Neil followed with Candy.

"Andy, what's going on? You didn't tell me they were starting chemo this morning. That's going to make him really sick." She didn't know if she was more upset because of what this would do to her son or the fact that Andy was deciding everything again.

He must have known, as he slid his arm around her shoulder and pulled her close. "It's going to be okay," he said. She wanted to slap his arm away, but at the same time she felt safe and supported with him standing beside her. He squeezed her shoulder, holding her a little tighter.

"Okay to talk with everyone here?" the doctor asked, gesturing toward Neil and Candy.

"Yes, they're family," Andy said.

"Well, as I said last night, the type of leukemia that

Gabriel has is not hereditary," the doctor began. "It's aggressive. The cells are invading the marrow and will spread very quickly to the spinal fluid, the spleen, the liver and the brain if we're not aggressive with our treatment. We need to hit it hard and fast. The chemo is going to make Gabriel very sick. He'll have to stay here, as his immune system is going to be destroyed. It's imperative we find a match for Gabriel now, and ideally we'll be able to harvest and freeze the donor sample."

"Wait, I was tested last night. I'm his mother. Shouldn't I be a perfect match?" Laura asked. She glanced up at Andy, and she knew, just by the hard set of his jaw, that he was holding on to something. "Andy?"

"You're not a match," Andy said. "We need a better match. A match he can only get from his biological relatives."

Laura stared up at him, trying to understand what he was talking about. Then it hit her, this awful feeling that she wasn't going to like what he said one bit. "So what are you saying, Andy? Please tell me you're not considering …"

"I have to, Laura. I'm sorry. I didn't want you to find out this way, but I'm going to find your parents and the kid who fathered Gabriel."

Her heart was pounding at the thought of Andy contacting her parents or, worse yet, Tyler. She didn't want to relive the humiliation, even though Andy knew everything she'd been through. She instantly felt guilty for thinking that way. She would do anything for Gabriel, and so would Andy, but she couldn't help but be embarrassed. Andy's cousin and his wife were listening, no doubt wondering what skeletons she had in her closet. She ached, thinking of what they must think of her.

The doctor was shaking his head, and Laura wondered why. She wanted to cry. Her emotions were hammering her good sense and turning her into a basket case, which she could have sworn she'd never been before. She was starting to wonder how much a person could really take before they snapped.

"We need to get each of them tested," the doctor said. "Wherever they are, we can make arrangements at a local hospital for testing and extraction of the marrow. Just let me know, and, as I said …"

"I know. Time is not on our side. I'll get on it," Andy said.

Neil stepped forward beside Andy and offered Laura a sympathetic smile. "What do we need to do? How can we help?" he asked, looking from Andy to the doctor.

"Gabriel is going to need someone to be with him while he goes through this," the doctor said. "We can keep him comfortable. Children are actually much stronger when dealing with this than most adults are. However, he's going to be scared, and …"

"He won't be alone. I'm not leaving my son," Laura snapped. "When are you starting?"

"Right away. Once we start the chemo, and kill all the cancer cells in the marrow, we need to move on to the stem cell transplant." The doctor took all of them in, and all Laura felt was nausea at the thought of what her son was going to have to go through. At the same time, she really didn't understand how bad it was going to get. She'd have given anything to be able to trade places with him.

"Wherever you need us, Candy and I are here to help," Neil said. He set his hand on Andy's shoulder and squeezed. "We need a plan. Let's figure this out and get a handle on what we'll do first." Neil took charge, all confidence. Candy slid comfortably and easily to his side as his arm hooked around her shoulder. "Let's get some coffee, clear our heads and we'll figure this out together."

Laura looked to Andy, who was looking so tired. She realized that having Neil here was probably the best thing for them; and, just maybe, having that one clear head would keep her and Andy from completely falling apart.

Chapter 17

Laura was an absolute mess. She had to keep turning her head so Gabriel wouldn't see her cry, but Andy could see how she kept wiping at her eyes. When the babies started fussing, he hoped Laura would take them out and nurse them; but he also knew she was in no shape to go off alone right now. Andy looked to Neil and the babies, hoping he understood. He also kind of hoped Neil's new wife, Candy, would step in and help; but she looked about as uncomfortable with Laura as Laura was with her.

"Oh, look at you!" Neil cooed as he squatted down to see the babies. Both were awake. "Now, which one is this? It's kind of hard to tell."

"That's Jeremy. He's the demanding one," Andy added as Neil scooped his son up. He was such a natural with babies, and so comfortable, too. "Laura?" Andy said.

She was sitting with Gabriel even though he was asleep again. She jerked her head up and then stood, her eyes red and her lids puffy. She started toward the baby Neil was holding—she seemed to be one step from falling apart.

"Laura, you need to get some sleep," Andy said. "Maybe you can take her home, Neil, Candy?"

"I'm not leaving, Andy," she said.

He knew he needed to get her to relax, but he also needed to be with Gabriel. He swept his hand through his hair and absently noticed how uncomfortable Candy was when Neil stepped toward her with the baby.

"Look at him, isn't he so cute?" Neil said. "It's the Friessen nose."

Candy smiled up at Neil but made no move to take Jeremy. After what she'd been through, losing her baby and undergoing an emergency hysterectomy on their wedding day, Andy had wondered whether his cousin's marriage was done. They truly loved each other, and both of them had climbed over a tremendous hurdle to find their way back to each other. Andy didn't know if he would have still married her. Children were important. The thought of his wife not being able to have his babies, of not having Chelsea and Jeremy … well, his cousin was a better man than he was.

"And the demanding Friessen attitude, too," Andy added, nodding at his son.

"Hmm, we are, at that, aren't we?" Neil said. The words should have lightened the mood in the room, but Laura was unmoved beside him.

"I'll take him. He's probably hungry," she said.

Neil set the baby in her arms and smiled at her. He was trying to ease her stress, but Laura, being Laura, was nervous, self-conscious and overtired. She wasn't about to relax. Neil gave Andy a look over Laura's head, his expression completely alert as he gestured to the door.

Andy nodded. "Laura, I'll be right back. Anyone want a coffee?"

Neil said something to Candy and kissed her on the

cheek. She smiled, touching his arm and nodding in response to whatever it was he'd said. In the hallway, Neil set his hand on Andy's shoulder and gave him a quick embrace. "You okay?" he asked.

Andy took a deep breath and raked both hands through his hair. "Just tired—this all came out of left field."

"Laura looks on edge, exhausted." Neil gestured to the room.

Andy could only see the side of his wife as she sat in the chair, probably to nurse his son. Candy moved away from the door. He couldn't make out what she was saying to Laura, but hopefully it was something that would draw her out of her shell. Anything to help.

"She didn't get any sleep last night, and she was at home alone with the babies," Andy said. "I couldn't do anything for her—I needed to be here for Gabriel. She's a wreck, and …"

"I can see that. I'm just glad you called. Mom and Dad said to call them if you want them to come, too. They'll be on the next flight out. Mom didn't want to get underfoot, especially since you just moved here."

"Appreciate it," Andy said. He'd been considering off and on whether to call them, too. His aunt and uncle needed to be told as well—but for now, just having Neil and Candy there was enough.

"Dad said to let him know if he can do anything at his end."

Andy just nodded to that. Although he would have liked to have Rodney and Becky here; having Neil meant a lot to him. Maybe it was just as well, as he started wondering where to put them. They had barely moved in, and they really weren't set up for guests.

"So, tell me about Laura's family," Neil said. "I understand they're not close. Actually, I don't know anything about them, Andy," he added as they lingered outside the room, far enough that Laura wouldn't be able to hear.

"I don't know Sue and George Parnell—and I never wanted to know them," Andy said. He didn't miss the mix of sympathy and shrewdness in Neil's expression. His cousin had a way of listening completely, taking in everything they said—and everything they didn't. That was probably why he was so successful at everything he did in business. In Andy's eyes, everything Neil touched turned to gold.

"It was hard for Laura, and I only know what she's told me," he began. "Just hearing how bad something was, is completely different from actually experiencing it. I saw how hard it was for her, alone with a baby. She'd just turned sixteen when she had Gabriel. She'd made a mistake. The kid who got her pregnant turned his back on her, and her parents threw her out. She struggled, working part-time jobs, living in shitholes. She wouldn't give him up. She loves him."

"Wow, admirable—and unfair. Wouldn't it have been easier to give him up to a family who could give him everything he needed?"

Andy was surprised Neil would say that, and he had to take a step back. "She loved him. He was hers. Would you have given up your kid?" he asked.

Neil didn't answer for a minute; then his expression changed to something dark and hard. Andy had never seen that before, and he wasn't sure what to make of it. "No, if I had a kid right now, he'd have everything, but I don't and Candy can't have any. There are so many couples looking to adopt a baby from a young mother like Laura. I can see the other side, where Gabriel wouldn't have had to struggle; where Laura could have gone on to college and had a life without suffering. Sorry," he added.

Andy crossed his arms and took in a side of Neil he really didn't like. "I hope you would never say that to Laura. She'd never forgive you, and I wouldn't, either—if you hurt her. She's had more than her share of pain in this lifetime, Neil, and if she had given up Gabriel, I wouldn't have met her, let alone married her. I'd probably be the same selfish prick I was."

Neil reached over and grabbed his shoulder. "Hey, I'm sorry, Andy. I didn't mean it like that, and I would never say that to your wife. I'm sorry about blurting it out now. It's just … I planned on having a family with Candy. In Mexico, we see so many hungry kids living in poverty, and it's jaded me. I notice it now, but I didn't mean to lay it on you. I like Laura; and I see that she loves her son. I know you love him, too. I can see that. I can see why you hate the idea of talking to her family after they abandoned her. You're going to call them, aren't you?"

"Yeah, and that kid who got her pregnant. It's just …" Andy wasn't sure he wanted to voice his fears, but in the back of his mind, the idea of someone else being Gabriel's father, being in his life, didn't sit right. A whole lot of what-ifs were starting to take shape.

"It's just what, Andy? What are you worried about? I can see you're tired. I can tell, because you're not hiding things well."

Andy sucked in a deep breath and ran his hands over his head again. "There are just too many loose ends. Legally, Gabriel is not mine. If something happened to Laura …" He hesitated. He didn't want to finish that thought. The thought that had been there all night as he sat alone in the hospital chair beside Gabriel's bed; watching the little boy he felt was his in every sense of the word—except in the eyes of the law. "I screwed up. With everything that happened... moving to Montana, I meant to take steps to legally adopt him."

"Well, first things first, Andy. You need to talk to these people. I'll go with you. I think you need someone objective. Someone who knows how to swing a deal and think fast on his feet."

"I can think fast and I've put together more deals than I can count," Andy snapped.

"Maybe so—but reverse the positions, Andy. This is your kid, and you're emotionally involved. I can bet you'd rather plant your fist in something or someone than have to sit down and be reasonable."

If he thought about it long enough, Andy was sure he would agree. However, Neil was being far more honest than he wanted.

Chapter 18

Laura was squeezed in the backseat of Andy's truck, in between Chelsea and Jeremy, in the spot where Gabriel usually sat. She had never sat back here and the view was surreal. She was so tired that her head ached.

Candy was in the passenger seat beside Neil, who had spoken to her only once, when keying the address into the GPS. He spoke with his wife, an easy conversation that flowed back and forth; though Laura wasn't really paying attention to what they said to each other. She didn't miss their linked hands, their fingers resting together on the center console.

"Laura, you all right back there?" Neil asked, and she met the amber sparkle of his eyes in the rear-view mirror. He was such a handsome man, so clean cut. He resembled Andy in many ways, and in many others he didn't. Her husband had a shrewdness she didn't believe Neil had.

Candy turned her head when she didn't answer. "You're tired, aren't you?"

"I am. My head hurts. I just don't know whether I'll be

able to sleep if I lie down," she said, wishing she was still back at the hospital—reliving in her mind how sick Gabriel had been when they left. After his first course of treatment, he had been wiped out, but had thrown up only once. He seemed to find comfort lying in Andy's arms. "They said there would be mouth sores, hair loss, nausea, vomiting, diarrhea and loss of appetite," Laura murmured, saying out loud what had been running through her mind over and over again.

Candy rustled in the front seat, leaning around the console. "Who said that?" she asked.

Laura realized they were both watching her; Neil in the rear-view mirror and Candy, who looked over to her husband and back at Laura again. "The doctor did, or was it the oncologist? Those are the side effects for Gabriel. How does he deserve this? It's not fair," she said. Her chest ached from the sorrow she'd been trying to bottle up and all the endless tears that kept flowing. Andy was tired, too, but he was handling it way better than she was. She rubbed her forehead and tucked her knotted hair behind her ears. She couldn't for the life of her force herself to smile or even make an effort through the agony. She had hoped never to feel this kind of pain again.

"It's going to be okay, Laura," Candy said. "Children handle things better than adults do, and he's going to get through this. He has you and Andy, and you love him. Having parents like you two is going to get him through this. You just have to believe he's going to be okay. It's one day at a time, Laura."

Laura didn't miss the way Neil responded when Candy spoke; running his thumb over their intertwined hands. Laura could only nod.

The sun was setting as they started up the incline to their new home and the familiar pickup that always stirred her anxiety came into view. "I forgot about Ladystar," she said. There was a horse trailer attached to the truck.

"Whose pickup is that?" Neil asked as he pulled up beside it. Just as Kim came around the house, leading Ladystar on her halter. "Who's the woman?" he added, and Candy glanced back at Laura.

"Kim, our neighbor," she said, wondering if she sounded as bitter to them as she did to her own ears. Candy turned her head ever so slowly toward Neil and they exchanged a look. Both turned to Laura before Neil stepped out of the truck. She couldn't make out what he was saying, but he was friendly; stepping right over to Kim and shaking her hand. She waved through the windshield at Laura.

Candy opened the back door. "I'll help you in with the babies," she said. She started to lift the car seat out when Neil approached from behind and set his hands on her hips, moving her aside and lifting Jeremy out.

"Candy, why don't you grab the bag from the gift shop?" he said, and Candy lifted a large plastic bag out along with her purse. Neil held out his hand to help Laura.

"I can take Chelsea," she said, reaching for the baby carrier.

"No, I've got her. You go on in with my wife. I'll bring both the babies, our luggage and anything else there is."

He was such a gentleman. That was something Andy would have said and done.

Laura stopped at the steps. "Hi, Kim. Thank you for taking care of Andy's horse." She was feeling bad for being so jealous of a woman who didn't have to be here and helping out the way she was.

"You're welcome, Laura. Glad to help. How's your little boy?" she asked as she loaded Ladystar in the trailer.

"Sick. He's started chemo. Andy's still with him."

Kim just nodded. "My prayers are with you and your family. Let me know if there's anything else I can do." She locked up the back door of the trailer.

"I know Andy has probably thanked you for taking his horse and for looking after her. It helps us more than you know; not having to worry about her being here all alone."

"She'll fit in fine at my place with my horses. She won't be lonely, and I'll keep her as long as you need," Kim said. Laura wondered if she'd picked up on all her jealous thoughts, because she didn't linger. She just offered a sympathetic smile, waved and slid into her truck before pulling away.

From the door behind her, Candy was watching. Laura started toward her, and an icy chill raced through her veins as soon as she touched the knob. She patted her pockets. "Oh, shit, I don't have keys." She touched her forehead and dug her nails in. "Dammit, I am so sorry."

"What's wrong?" Neil called out.

"Laura doesn't have keys," Candy said.

"I can't believe how stupid I am! I didn't even think to bring any keys with me. Andy has the keys to the house. I'm sorry, we're going to have to drive all the way back to the hospital." She wanted to cry, and she felt horrible, as if she was responsible for this entire mess.

"Laura, it's okay. I've got Andy's keys," Neil assured her. He set the babies down and pulled the keys from his pocket. "This one?" He held up a silver house key.

"Yes, that's the one," she said.

He shoved it in the deadbolt and opened the door. Laura moved ahead of Candy into the dim house. She turned on the kitchen light and shivered. The house was cold, but there was no heat and hadn't been since yesterday. Candy put a bag on the table, and Neil set down both baby carriers.

"Candy?" he said, gesturing to the babies.

She nodded. "It's okay, I'm here."

He leaned down and kissed her—Laura had to look away. "I'll grab the bags," he said before stepping out the door.

The babies still slept in their car seats. Laura started toward them, about to unbuckle Chelsea so she could put her in her crib, when Candy pulled a breast pump from the bag. Laura was a little confused. Maybe that was what Candy saw when she said, "I'm sorry, but Neil bought three." She pulled all of them from the bag. "He wasn't sure which one was the best, and I'm not much help in that area."

Laura reached for the blue box. "I'm sure any one of these will be fine. Why is he buying …"

"For you," Candy said before she could finish. "It's just the way he is. I don't know if your husband is the same, but Neil tends to take charge, take over and arrange, handle and deal …" she said. For the first time that Laura could remember, she burst out laughing. She was met with a bright smile from Candy. "Well, we can't help with the twins unless you provide the milk, and you don't even need to tell him which ones you don't like."

"Thank you, Candy. Really," Laura said. She didn't know the woman well, but she was family. There was something genuine about her that she couldn't help but like.

Chapter 19

Andy listened to the ringing once, then twice, as he paced in the empty visitors' room on the pediatric floor.

"Hello?" A younger boy's voice answered the phone, and Andy wondered if it was one of Laura's brothers. There was something about the voice that was similar to hers.

"Hello, could I speak to George Parnell?" Andy said.

"Dad!"

He listened to the boy call out. He heard a clatter of dishes in the background. There were other voices, and a woman asked the boy who it was. He figured that had to be Laura's mother.

"Hello?" a man said into the phone.

"Is this George Parnell?" Andy asked.

"Yeah, yeah, who's calling?" the man asked. He said something to someone in the background that Andy couldn't make out.

"My name is Andy Friessen. Your daughter, Laura, is my wife," he said. There was silence on the other end.

"Give me a minute," the man said. There was rustling, and then it became quieter as, Andy guessed, a door closed. "Laura is married? Why? She's so young. Is she all right?"

This didn't sound like a man who hated his daughter. There was concern there. "She's fine. The reason I'm calling is Gabriel, our little boy. He's very sick."

"Gabriel? You have a child?" The man was hesitant on the other end.

"We have three, two of them are newborn twins. Gabriel is the little boy she had when she was pregnant at fifteen—when you asked her to leave."

"I didn't know his name," the man said. "So she kept him."

Andy wasn't sure what to make of his response. "Yes, she loves him. I love him. But he's very sick right now. He has leukemia—and the only way to save his life is with a bone marrow transplant. It needs to be a perfect tissue match, which can only come from family, but Laura's not a match."

"I'm so sorry to hear that, but I don't understand how I can help," the man said.

Andy felt the first alarm bell go off. If that had been him, and Laura was his daughter, nothing could have kept him from being here. Making sure his daughter and his grandson were taken care of, that his grandson had everything he needed. Hell, if his daughter got pregnant, he'd never toss her out—though he would kill the boy who did it. Andy couldn't understand anything about this man.

"You're his grandfather...We need you and your wife, as well as Laura's brothers, to be tested for a match," Andy said. His voice had become so humble, that it made him ill to suck up to someone this way. He ground his teeth, wanting nothing more than to reach through the phone and shake the man.

The man took a breath on the other end. "I'll have to talk to my wife."

"Seriously? I'm confused on what your hesitation is. This is a little boy who's done nothing to you. I don't understand why you're not all over this. Do you hate your daughter that much?" Andy said. He was shaking, and he didn't realize how loud he had been until a nurse passing in the hallway poked her head in and gestured for him to quiet down.

"You sound very angry and I'm not going to get into this with you on the phone. So I think I'll bid you a good night," the man said, and then the line went dead.

Andy stared in disbelief at the phone, unable to believe this man had actually hung up on him. He threw his cell phone at the wall, shattering it.

Chapter 20

Laura wandered into the living room in her white robe, her damp hair brushed back. She had taken a long bath and almost fallen asleep after Neil insisted that she take care of herself. It hadn't taken too much convincing. She ached, and had longed for a bath. She just wanted to sit and think...To relax. Neil was dominant, in a charming sort of way. He was different from her husband, although he enjoyed telling her what to do, too. He wasn't a man to take no for an answer. Surprisingly, Candy didn't seem to pay him much mind.

Laura was surprised to see Candy holding Chelsea in the warm living room; rocking her by the fire. She stood in the shadows and just watched. Neil was beside her, holding Jeremy and telling Candy how to hold the baby. Laura could tell how nervous and uncertain Candy was feeling, but she was still willing to try. Then they noticed her.

"Hey, how are you feeling?" Neil asked.

She stepped into the living room barefoot. Candy appeared to stiffen, uncertain with the baby. Laura had never pictured Candy as the mothering type.

"I'm good. Are they hungry?" she asked as she started into the living room, feeling the welcoming heat from the fire.

"This one is. Your demanding son—who's bigger than his sister, from taking more than his share." Neil looked so comfortable holding the baby. It wasn't lost on her that he would make a good father. "Laura, did you get a chance to try out one of the breast pumps?" he asked.

Immediately, her face burned in embarrassment. "No, I've never used one."

"Well, Candy and I need to be able to feed these two to help out. You need to use them, start storing your milk. You can take one of them with you to the hospital to use, and then you can leave the babies with us while you stay with Gabriel."

She didn't know what to say to that, but it made a lot of sense. Actually, it was a relief to have the option, because she didn't want to leave Gabriel. Right now, she wanted nothing more than to race back to the hospital and be with her son. "Okay, let me feed Jeremy, and then I'll use the pump. I'd like to go back to the hospital," she said.

"Yeah, I'll take you in the morning after you get some sleep."

She firmed her lips. She couldn't believe Neil was making her wait but, then again, her husband had almost ordered him to take her and the babies home. To make sure she laid down and got some sleep. It seemed now, that he was going to follow what Andy said to a T. "I would feel better if I went back tonight. I'm not going to get much sleep here, lying awake, worrying about my son."

Neil set the baby in her arms and slid his hand on her back, guiding her to another easy chair by the woodstove. She wasn't really comfortable nursing in front of Candy and Neil and wondered if they realized.

"Hey, feed your son, but I'm not taking you back tonight. Andy will call if there's any change. Laura, you're about to fall over." Neil squatted down in front of her. "You're not going to be any use to Gabriel, or the babies, if you don't get some sleep. Besides, your husband would kill me if I let you go back tonight." Neil's cell phone started ringing. He pulled it from the leather pouch clipped to his belt, glanced at the screen, then turned away. "Hey, how's it going?" he said. When he turned around, he glanced at Laura. She wondered who it was. "That doesn't sound too good. Do you want me to come in?"

Laura could feel her Spidey senses tingling; the hairs coming alive on the back of her neck. She knew it had to be Andy by the way Neil watched her. Something must be wrong. Jeremy fussed and pulled on her housecoat, trying to open it and get his dinner. Being unable to relax was not helping. Neil gestured for her to stay put.

"Do you want me to call? I'm pretty persuasive," he said. He moved away, listening to whatever Andy was saying. "Okay, call me after you talk to him, then. No, she's fine. She's going to bed. We'll be back in the morning. You, too," he said before hanging up while staring straight at Laura. "Your husband," he said. He looked to Candy, who was still rocking Chelsea, looking a little more comfortable. Chelsea was such an easy baby.

"Neil, what's going on? Why is my husband not talking to me?" she asked. All this over-protectiveness was beginning to tick Laura off. She felt as though she was being kept out of the loop.

"He called your parents...Mainly your dad. It didn't go well," Neil replied.

There, for a second, she wasn't sure she'd heard right. Then she realized what he'd said. She was mortified that Neil had heard anything about her parents and what had happened when she was a teen. She shut her eyes when it registered just how badly they still must hate her.

"Wow, so I suppose my husband told you all the gory details," she snapped, finally settling Jeremy on her breast. She could feel both Candy and Neil watching, but she refused to meet their gaze. She was so tired of everyone judging her.

"Hey, Laura, give yourself a break," Candy said. "Whatever problems your parents have are their issues. Whatever happened, you were a child and should have had your parents' support. Shame on them, Laura, not you. Neil, are you helping?" she added.

When Laura glanced up and took in the exchange between Neil and Candy, she wondered what was going on. "Apparently my husband doesn't like to share what he's thinking. Neil, I want you to tell me right now," Laura insisted, covering her breast with her hand, feeling far too exposed in front of Neil.

"I think I should talk to your parents. Andy would just as soon … well, you know how your husband feels about your parents. He planned to never meet them or have them in your lives. I think he'd like to get your dad alone right about now, which is definitely not a good idea with the way he's feeling. Candy's right, by the way," he added. "Your dad's a prick. Any father who wouldn't look after his child … I'm sorry, but I have no use for him."

Candy frowned, looking at her husband as if she wanted to pull him aside. "He's right, Laura," she said. "As much as it pains me to admit, Neil's probably right about talking with your father. He's very persuasive, and he would be the best person to talk with your parents."

"I think I should talk to them," Laura said. "After all, they are my parents. I don't want to drag you into the middle of this, Neil. My husband should've been talking to me about this."

"Well, I think your husband thinks differently, Laura. You really need to let us handle this," Neil said. It sounded a little sharp, and Laura wasn't sure how to respond. He was family, but she barely knew him. Yet he was stepping in and acting on her husband's behalf. She looked at Candy, who just shook her head; irritation rolling off of her.

"Neil, Laura has to be hungry," she said. "I know I am."

He appeared distracted, maybe even irritated with her. Laura was aware she could push Andy's buttons at times, and obviously she pushed Neil's, too. "I'll go whip up some dinner," he said.

"I'm actually kind of tired, so don't make anything for me," she said. "I think I'm just going to go to bed. I'll sleep in Gabriel's room. You two take mine." She started to stand before remembering she hadn't made the bed. "I'm sorry, I'll have to put clean sheets on the bed for you."

"Laura, it's fine," Candy said. "We'll take care of it. You have enough to do, but you have to eat. Neil, just make her some eggs."

"Candy's right, Laura. You're feeding two babies. You have to eat something. I'll put something together."

Thankfully, he disappeared into the kitchen, because Laura wasn't sure she could have been polite much longer. When she looked up, Candy was watching her.

"Try to forgive my husband," she said. "One of the biggest obstacles I had to get over was the way Neil just rushes in and fixes things without discussing his plans. Do you know that your husband absolutely terrifies me? As domineering as Neil can be, he has nothing on your husband."

That comment had Laura smiling. "Yeah, Andy's definitely all that, but I love him so much that it hurts sometimes. He'd never allow anyone to hurt us. I think he'd kill a man with his bare hands if he ever did anything like that. And he loves my son like his own. I never expected that, because when he married me, it was more out of obligation, to be the hero. We've worked through a lot. I don't know where we'd be without him," she said, and then she just stopped talking. She didn't want to speak anymore. She didn't know what she wanted.

"Laura, the omelette's ready." Neil poked his head around the corner, and Jeremy, who'd fallen fast asleep on her breast, slipped off.

Fast asleep—boy, how she envied that.

Chapter 21

Andy jumped when a hand touched his shoulder. His neck ached, and he blinked in the dim room, staring up at Laura, who was looking way better than he felt. Neil was behind her, and he touched her coat. He didn't see the babies.

"Hey, how are you? How's Gabriel?" Laura asked.

Andy took in the huddled form of his little boy, fast asleep on the bed. "Surprisingly well. He's handling this like a trooper. Where're the twins?"

"With Candy at home," Neil said. "They were still sleeping when we left. I'll head back and give her a hand. I thought I would drag you back with me."

"Laura, you're nursing the babies. You can't stay here without them," Andy said. He was so tired he couldn't even attempt to sound reasonable.

"Your cousin took care of that," she said. She lifted a breast pump from the big purse she carried, which always had extra diapers and wipes for the babies.

"You bought my wife a breast pump?" Andy said. He couldn't believe Neil would do that.

"Actually, your cousin bought three," Laura interrupted.

"Well, have you taken a look at all the brands? How do you know which one is the best? Anyway, how are we going to help unless we can feed the babies? I'm pretty sure you're not doing formula."

"Hell, no. Not for my kids. I should have thought of it myself," Andy added, because he couldn't believe Neil had been the one to suggest it.

Laura leaned down and kissed Andy on the lips. She pulled away just far enough that he could see she had something on her mind. "Why didn't you tell me you were calling my parents?" she said. "I should have been with you when you did." She touched his cheek and then set her bag on the other chair.

He just watched her and wondered how she'd react to knowing her father couldn't make a decision even if his grandson's life depended on it. No, he had to go talk to her mother. The fact was that he wasn't racing down here to be with her, to save his grandson… He'd simply hung up on Andy, who had pushed with everything he had. He didn't want Laura to be hurt any more. He'd rather have her angry at him than to see the shadow of that pain her parents had buried in her with a hatchet, cutting into her heart.

"No, it took everything I had in me to call them," he said. "You have enough on your plate. I'll handle your parents. I don't want you to have to deal with them, Laura."

"Andy, they're my parents, my problem."

He couldn't believe she'd said that. "Well, that's where you're wrong, sweetheart. You're my wife, my responsibility—therefore, they're my problem."

She looked away, and he wasn't sure why she looked so

bothered. "What about Tyler?" she asked. "Are you planning on calling him, too?"

There was a knock on the door. "Hi, Laura," said a male voice he wasn't familiar with.

Andy was out of that chair, standing behind his wife, who stared at a tall, slender young man with blue eyes the shade of indigo, reddish short hair and a narrow face that looked down at Laura with a familiarity Andy didn't like.

"Tyler," Laura said. Her voice sounded strange, as if it was a struggle to get the name out.

Andy stared for a moment at the young man who had shut the door in her face so long ago, when she needed him most. Andy reached out his hand. "I'm Andy Friessen, Laura's husband—and Gabriel's father," he added. Everyone looked to the little boy in the bed. Tyler shook Andy's hand and then glanced down at Laura again.

"You look good, Laura," he said.

Andy moved closer beside her, putting his arm around her and pulling her against him. He was letting this punk know darn well that Laura was his, off limits. Tyler gazed at Gabriel, who was rustling in bed.

"Andy," he called out in such a weak voice.

"Hey, right here, bud," Andy said. Gabriel opened his eyes and took in Neil, standing so quiet, then Tyler. Laura scooted by Andy and went to Gabriel's side, giving all of them her back.

"Hi, honey. How are you feeling?" she asked, brushing back his bangs. Andy moved closer behind her and reached around, setting his hand on Gabriel's head.

"I want to go home," Gabriel said.

"I know you do, honey. Soon. The doctor just has to make you all better first," Laura said. When she glanced up at Andy, he'd have to have been a fool to miss the pained expression she gave him. Well, hell, he hadn't expected Tyler to show up here. The kid should have gone to a local hospital.

"Is that Gabriel?" Tyler said as he stepped around the bed, and Laura glanced up at Andy again. Andy watched Tyler, hoping the kid wouldn't move any closer. He wanted him out of here and far away from his son.

"Yeah," Andy said. "Can I talk to you outside?"

Tyler smiled down at Gabriel and seemed to really take him in with an interest Andy didn't particularly like.

"Tyler," he prompted again as Tyler stepped closer still and brushed his knuckles against the bedding next to Gabriel's foot. Andy had to fight against every caveman instinct he had not to grab Tyler and drag him out. He didn't want him seeing Gabriel or having anything to do with him. The way Laura was watching Tyler... He could tell she was thrown. This wasn't how he'd planned it, and this wasn't something he wanted between them.

Tyler glanced his way and stepped away from the bed, following Andy into the hall, Neil flanking him. "I didn't expect him to look so helpless. He has my mother's eyes, and his expression …"

"Tyler, thanks for coming so quickly. This is my cousin Neil," Andy said. Struggling with the highs and lows that came with a lack of sleep was making him punchy. He thought he'd been clear that Gabriel was his son when he'd called Tyler last night.

Neil shook his hand, and Tyler appeared less confident than he had been when he stepped into his son's hospital room. Good! Andy wanted him nervous, off balance, scared shitless. He didn't want Tyler to confuse this with an opportunity to get to know the kid he'd fathered.

"Good to meet you," Neil added.

"I called Tyler last night and filled him in on Gabriel. He said he'd get tested to see if he's a match," Andy said, because he'd never called his cousin back after talking to Tyler. He was still surprised that, to his credit, the kid hadn't hesitated to say yes after Andy tracked him down and called him at his university dorm in Missoula.

"So what do I do now?" he asked.

Andy glanced at the nurses' station. "Let me just get a hold of Doctor Siegel and have him set up the tests. What happened to having the test done in Missoula?" he asked. It wasn't just curiosity that made this kid skip school and drive all this way for some son he'd never met.

"I don't know, really. I got to thinking about how I let Laura down. Not a day goes by that I don't think about the baby, whether she had him, what happened to him. The next thing I knew, I drove past the hospital in Missoula and just kept driving until I pulled into the parking lot here." He offered a smile as if Andy should appreciate what he'd done. Andy didn't miss the hard look Neil leveled at him. Yeah, this kid could be trouble. What-ifs sometimes led to things that wouldn't be good for any of them.

"Let's find the doctor and get Tyler tested," Neil urged, setting his hand on Tyler's shoulder.

Andy flagged down a nearby nurse. "Can you page Doctor Siegel?" he asked, but she pointed with her pen.

"He's on rounds, right there."

Doctor Siegel approached, looking fresh in neatly pressed slacks, a green dress shirt and a fashionable striped tie, his white doctor's coat pulled overtop. "Andy, how was Gabriel through the night?" He asked, taking a chart from the nurse and opening it.

"He slept most of the night. He was sick, though. How much worse is it going to get?"

"Hard to tell, Andy. Everyone responds differently, some sicker than others. I'll see how he's holding up after today's round. We have to do a couple, but we'll watch him closely."

"This is Tyler," Andy said. "I spoke with you about him. He fathered—he's the kid I told you about who fathered Gabriel. He should be a biological match."

Doctor Siegel took in the clean-cut features of Tyler and extended his hand. "So you're Gabriel's father," he said.

"I'm Gabriel's father," Andy snapped. "Let's be clear: Tyler is not his father, and there is a difference."

He was being a real prick, and he knew it. Maybe that was why Neil was giving him a warning look. If Andy had been rested and in control of his emotions, he would have seen the danger signs.

"I think what my cousin is trying to say is that he married Laura and is Gabriel's father. A father is someone who is there for his son, raises him, loves him, and will move every obstacle to protect him," Neil said. "Tyler, we're so grateful you're willing to help Gabriel as his biological father, but we know you didn't want anything to do with him. Laura did it all alone until she met Andy. Brave girl. She's raised a fine boy," Neil added.

"Well, I'm not proud of what I did. I was scared. I was just a kid, too. I didn't want my parents to find out. I'm here now, and if I could go back to that day … well, I don't know, but I think I would handle things differently. There isn't a day that's gone past that I haven't wondered what happened to my child, whether it was a boy or a girl. She named him Gabriel. I used to joke to Laura all the time about how if I had a kid, I'd name him after the Archangel Gabriel. He was my favorite. I can't believe she remembered."

Andy wanted to wipe the smug, wistful look off his

face. He wasn't sure what to say in that moment, but he'd sure like to pull Laura aside and have a few words with her.

"Why don't I get you set up? We'll get you tested to see if you're a match," the doctor said, interrupting the direction the conversation was going, which was nowhere Andy wanted to go.

Tyler shrugged and shuffled his feet. He started to follow the doctor but then stopped in front of Andy. "Thank you for calling me and letting me know about my son," he said. He held out his hand to shake Andy's, and for a moment Andy considered violence. He had his arms crossed so tightly that it was Neil who finally stepped around and took Tyler's hand, patting his shoulder and turning him to follow the doctor.

"Thank you again. Doctor Siegel, how long does a test like this usually take?" Neil asked.

"I'll put a rush on it. Give it a few hours," he replied.

Andy just stood there and watched as Tyler walked away with the doctor, and Neil returned to his side.

"Andy, are you thinking there might be a problem here?" Neil asked, something that had been going through his mind since Tyler walked into Gabriel's hospital room.

"Yeah. I asked him to go to his local hospital to get tested. I'd already had Doctor Siegel call down there and make arrangements. He wasn't supposed to show up here."

"How did he know where Gabriel was?" Neil asked.

"I'm obviously slipping—I told him which hospital. Is it my imagination, or is his interest in Gabriel beyond being helpful?"

Neil was watching the hallway where Tyler had disappeared. "Do you want me to take care of this, make sure we have no problems here?"

"Let's wait for the test to come back, see if he's a match, but I don't want him around Gabriel or Laura. I want to make sure whatever's going through Tyler's mind, suddenly becoming a good ol' pop to my kid … We need to shatter that illusion right now, whatever it takes."

"Mister Friessen," the nurse interrupted him, "we're about ready to take Gabriel down for his next treatment."

Andy rubbed his head, trying to hold everything together for his son, for Laura, for everyone. "Yeah. I'll be right there. Just give me a minute." He let out a breath as he looked at his cousin.

"When was the last time you got some sleep?" Neil asked. "And I'm not talking about napping in a chair, off and on. I'm talking real sleep."

He just shook his head. "Can't be helped, Neil. As soon as we have some answers, as soon as we know more about a match, then I'll get some sleep. I can't leave him right now. I can't. If this was your kid, would you?"

He regretted it as soon as he saw the darkened expression on Neil's face.

"I'm sorry. I didn't mean it like that. I'm just tired, you know."

"Don't worry about it," Neil said. "I do know, because I wouldn't leave either—not for anything."

Chapter 22

Laura was still reeling from seeing Tyler. She hadn't had a moment alone with Andy to talk to him. How could he call Tyler and have him show up here? Because he thought it was best? He should have told her. That was what husbands and wives did. They talked to each other. His domineering attitude was getting really old.

Laura was standing beside Andy in the hallway, just the two of them, with Doctor Siegel. Neil had gone home to get Candy and to bring the babies in. Laura had been pumping milk, when she could, and storing it in bottles while in the patient and family lounge.

"So, as I said, Tyler is a better match than you, Laura; but not the perfect match we hoped for," Siegel said.

"Well, that was a waste of time," Andy said angrily, nearly biting off the doctor's head. Laura could see, as he stepped away, running his hands through his hair, that he was reaching the end of his rope. She didn't like having Tyler anywhere near Gabriel. She'd been freaking out inside ever since she saw that soft expression he leveled at Gabriel. The one people got when they cared for someone.

"Laura, you still have family," the doctor said. "Whatever the situation is, you need to talk to them and get them tested. I can't stress the urgency enough." The doctor gave them a meaningful look and then walked away, stopping at the nurses' station to speak with a nurse and reach for a chart.

"Andy." Laura went to touch him, but he pulled away and gave her a look as if she had done something wrong. He could be such a hard-ass sometimes. To get on the wrong side of him, was not something she ever wanted again. It hurt, and that simple motion felt like a rejection. "Did I do something?" she asked. She set her hand on her chest and didn't try to touch him again.

"Why didn't you tell me you named Gabriel for Tyler? Chose a name he wanted? How could you, after what that prick did to you?"

She watched as he walked in front of her and waited for her to say something. It took a moment, and then another, for her to recall why she'd given him that name. "Yes, it's true Tyler always talked about Gabriel, the great archangel, deliverer of messages," she said. "I've also heard that if the solution to a problem comes to mind, Archangel Gabriel is there. I may have named him Gabriel, but it wasn't because of Tyler—it was because Gabriel means 'no fear.' It fit. You should have told me you called Tyler!" she snapped back at him. She stepped toward him, jabbing a finger at his chest, "I'm so tired of your heavy-handed approach. How do you think I felt, standing there in my son's room, when Tyler walked in. The way he looked at him … do you have any idea what you're stirring up? Why would you bring him here?"

Andy wasn't looking at her like a man wronged anymore. He appeared so tired, as if he was carrying the weight of the world on his shoulders. "I didn't intend for him to come here. I swear, Laura. I called him last night at his dorm. He's in Missoula, going to school. I told him to go to the medical center there. Doctor Siegel even called ahead so they'd be expecting him. I was just as surprised as you were when he walked in." He didn't try to touch her but set his hands on his hips. "I'm doing the best I can; and I'm sorry, but I don't want that guy anywhere around you or Gabriel. I don't want you talking to him."

"Well, Andy, if you're not going to consult me …" She was so mad she had to stop herself before making a threat she didn't mean.

"What, we're done?" he said. "Is that what you were going to say?"

"Hey, you two, stop it," Neil said as he approached, carrying both babies. Candy was behind him. "You two have a very sick kid in that bed. You're both exhausted, and you're both making decisions no parent should have to make. Seriously, you want to start shouting stupid threats at each other? You two need to sit down together and talk."

"Neil …" Candy gestured to the door. "Laura, Gabriel is sick."

Andy was ahead of Laura as he reached Gabriel's bedside, lifting him and setting a basin under him so he could throw up in the bowl. He had vomit on his blanket, and he was so pale. Candy went and got one of the nurses while Laura raced into the bathroom and wet a washcloth, hurrying around the other side and wiping his face when he finished.

"Oh no," the nurse said as she peered into the room. "I'll get him some clean bedding and another gown. I'll get him something for the nausea, too." She hurried away.

Laura's hand was shaking as she touched Gabriel's forehead, sweeping his hair back. Andy and Laura started to take off his soiled gown but had to stop because of the

IV bag. The nurse returned a few seconds later, set a blanket and gown on the chair, and then fed the IV bag through the armhole.

A few moments later, when Gabriel was all cleaned up, Andy wrapped him in a clean blanket and lifted him while the nurse put clean bedding on the bed. Gabriel fussed under the bright lights, so Candy turned them off, dimming the room. When Jeremy fussed and grunted as if he was quite put out, being forgotten and left strapped into his carrier, Laura hissed in frustration and unbuckled him. For the first time that she could remember, she was torn between Gabriel and her babies. When she looked over at Andy, his expression was one she hadn't seen before: It was love, hurt, and something so fragile it touched a place inside her heart she didn't think anyone could ever touch. It was an understanding that this situation, could either finish them—or bring them closer together.

Chapter 23

"I still don't think this is a good idea," Andy said. He was behind the wheel, driving down the highway toward Arlington.

After a long talk in the hospital as Gabriel slept; Andy and Laura had agreed the best course of action was to go see Laura's parents. What surprised Andy more than anything was that Neil had backed Laura up; saying that taking Laura and the twins were the best solution. Candy, while holding his daughter, had added that Laura needed to be included. She needed to look her parents in the eyes, to stand up to them. There were a whole lot of things that needed to be settled with Andy beside her. Candy and Neil said that they would stay with Gabriel. So, after a few hours of sleep at home, Andy and Laura had hit the highway at dawn.

"Andy, do you think I want to walk up to their door, knock on it like a stranger and ask them for something? Do you have any idea how terrified I am to have my parents say what a horrible person I am? How I let them down, disappointed them and ruined their reputation? Do you think I want to have to listen again about how I was responsible for damaging my father's standing in the church? Maybe they'll decide to just shut the door in my face." When she looked over at him, her face was flushed and she looked absolutely terrified; as if she'd hit rock bottom. He'd seen that look once before on her face.

"I'm not going to allow anyone to talk to you that way. I just won't, Laura. They'll treat you with respect." He didn't finish his thought: If they didn't, he'd become their worst enemy. "Laura, let me do the talking, okay?"

She firmed her lips, fighting to hold herself together. She blew out a breath. "How do you think Gabriel is doing?"

"He's holding on, Laura. He's a fighter. He's strong. He's going to get through this. Let's just finish this with your parents. Let's find a match for our boy."

The drive from Columbia Falls to Arlington should have taken nine hours. With Andy driving, they made it in just under eight; even with a few brief stops to feed the babies. By the time they reached the outskirts of the community, the babies had other ideas. Mainly, that they weren't about to spend one more minute strapped into their baby seats. With both of them screaming, Andy pulled over at a local hotel and helped Laura change diapers; then held one baby while she nursed the other.

"We should grab something to eat," Andy said, taking in Laura's slender figure. She'd been picking at her food like a bird for days, and she had to eat to keep her milk up.

"We should, but I'd really like to get this over with. I'm not going to be able to relax or eat anything until we talk to them."

Laura was right—he was just as keyed up as she was, and it was getting late. The last thing Andy wanted to do was park in a hotel for the night and waste another day. If their tactics worked, they'd be gone in the morning. It was dinnertime now, and the darkness had just begun to set in. He could just feel it. It was a good time for them to show up on the doorstep.

Laura guided him through each turn to her parents' house. The closer they got, the harder it was to hold herself together. He reached across and took her hand when he turned down her street. The babies were starting to fuss more and more.

"That's it, the white house," she said. "Oh my God, they still have the yellow Volkswagen." She set her hand over her chest, her eyes glued to the two-story home. It was white with blue trim. Everything appeared neat and tidy in this upscale suburban community. A yellow Volkswagen beetle from the '70s was parked in the driveway, a midsize dark green minivan parked behind it. Lights were on inside the house, and it had just started to rain. Andy parked in front and had just turned off the engine when a teenager looked out the window, obviously interested in who was parking in front of his house.

"Oh my God, Andy, I think that's Chad. He was only eight when I left," Laura said. She was staring out that window as if her life depended on it. He couldn't help wondering what was racing through her mind. She appeared to be holding on to everything and was so tightly wound that he didn't think she'd relax even if he tried to hold her.

"Hey, do you want to wait here?" he asked. He touched her shoulder, and he could tell she wanted to dive over the armrest and into his arms.

She looked at him, the terror widening her eyes, but she shook her head. "No. I'll beg them if I have to. I swear to God, I will. They won't chase me away even though I'm terrified. I can do this with you. I can do this for Gabriel."

Andy looked past her as a man joined the boy at the window, watching them. "Well, it's now or never," he said, and he opened his door and stepped out into the cold drizzle, walking around the truck to get his wife.

ANDY CARRIED Chelsea while Laura carried a bundled Jeremy in her arms up the narrow path to the front door. Laura looked good, although a little tired. She wore a fur-lined leather bomber jacket, new jeans, and his ring, with a rock and setting that screamed money. He wanted her parents to see that she didn't need them; and he wanted to cram in their faces how well their daughter had done. She wasn't a nobody. They'd only reached the front step when the door flew open, held by a balding older man. Andy could see the resemblance to Laura in his eyes, but it was the boy behind him who shouted, "Laura!" and pushed past the man, throwing his arms around Laura and the baby.

Jeremy fussed from being crowded, and Laura looked to Andy. The boy was almost as tall as her, his arms around her neck. He had the same blond hair.

"Where have you been? I've missed you so much. Brian, Laura's here!" he yelled out behind him.

Andy didn't miss her father's expression. He had been shocked at first, but now Andy was positive he saw some care there. Her father took in the sight of the babies, and before he could say anything, a compact woman about Laura's height, with neat, dark hair cut in a very short style, appeared behind him. Her face was the same shape as Laura's, and the expression on her face was one of shock before something hardened, as if she'd suddenly remembered she was supposed to be angry at her daughter.

"Chad, come in here right now," she said in a sharp tone.

A tall, gangly boy who was a head taller than his dad appeared. His eyes widened, and he started around his parents. "Laura, where have you been?"

"No, Brian." Laura's mother went to stop him, but he gave her one of those defiant teenage looks and shrugged off her hand.

"Mister and Missus Parnell, we'd like to speak with you. We've driven a long way," Andy said.

"Hi." Chad lifted his hand, shuffling from one foot to the other, grinning up at Andy. "Laura, are you married?" he said, sounding so happy to see his sister.

"I am, Chad. This is my husband, Andy. Andy, that good-looking tall guy is my brother Brian. I can't believe how tall you are! And this is my mom and dad." She took a breath and said, "Mom, Dad, I'd really appreciate it if you would give us a moment."

Damn, Andy was proud of the way she stood tall before her parents and spoke in such a strong, clear voice. Snuggling Chelsea in his one arm, he set his other around Laura, holding her against him. When she looked up at him, he could have sworn the timid fear he'd seen earlier had started to vanish.

"Of course, come in," George said, gesturing to the hallway behind him and stepping back from the door, allowing them inside.

Andy didn't miss the sharp look he gave his wife or the way Sue kept glancing at the babies, both awake. Jeremy was cooing. Chad didn't seem ready to leave Laura's side, as he hooked his hand around her arm. Her father shut the door and shoved both of his hands in his pockets, bouncing on the balls of his feet.

Andy had to tell himself he'd handled tougher situations than this in business, so this should have been easy. But it wasn't; he tended to lose all rational thought around anyone who could hurt someone he loved. Somehow, as he rubbed Laura's arm, he extended his hand to her father to shake it. "We haven't formally met," he said. "Andy Friessen."

He wondered if the man was going to snub him, as he stood still for a few seconds before finally pulling his hand from his pocket and taking Andy's. "George Parnell." He glanced at Laura. "You have another baby. Two, I see."

"We have twins, a boy and a girl, six weeks old," Andy said. "This is Chelsea, and Laura is holding Jeremy," he added, taking in Sue's interest and hesitation. Boy, Laura's parents weren't about to make this easy.

"You look good, sis," Brian said. He smiled up at Andy when he stepped in front of his mom; both boys taking in Jeremy, who had quite the frown as he looked up at the boys gawking at him. It was hilarious, and Andy would have laughed if this had been any other time.

"Dad, look at him! That's your nose, isn't it?" Brian pointed out. He winked at Laura when her father leaned in and took a closer look at his grandson. Yeah, right. Not even close, Andy thought. That was the Friessen nose.

"Oh, yeah, he does. Kind of looks like you two when you were babies," George said lightly.

"So how have you been?" Sue said without giving Andy a second look.

"I'm good, Mom." Laura didn't add anything else, probably because the tension was absolutely crushing with all this civility. It was as if she and Andy were strangers who had just shown up on the doorstep and were trying to sell them something.

"Look, we've driven all day to talk to you," Andy said. "When I spoke with you on the phone, George, I told you how sick Gabriel was, and …"

"Who's Gabriel?" Brian blurted out, looking between his mom and dad. "You knew where Laura was, but you said you had no idea why she'd left. Did you lie?" Brian yelled.

George just let out a sigh. "Come on, let's go sit in the living room," he said. He gestured to Andy and then went toward his son, most likely to calm him down, but it wasn't working. Brian stood face to face with his father. "I didn't know where Laura was," George said. "Let's just go in and sit down."

Laura gave Andy a worried look, but he set his hand on her lower back and followed her into an average square room with a blue cloth sofa and loveseat. There was a dark brown easy chair in the corner, which looked like something from the '80s. It had definitely seen better days. There were lamps on the side tables and photos on the walls. Andy did notice a family portrait from when Laura was a kid, standing beside Chad, who couldn't have been more than Gabriel's age.

George went right to the worn easy chair, obviously his domain. Laura moved to the sofa with Andy beside her. Her younger brother sat on the other side, still holding on to her as if he was afraid she would leave at any moment.

"Do you want to hold him?" Laura said as Chad touched Jeremy's foot, which he had kicked out from under the blanket.

"I don't know if that's such a good idea," Sue said from where she sat across from them. She was sitting so straight, her legs together, tucked properly to the side.

Andy was surprised as he watched the exchange between Laura and her brother. Neither appeared to pay their mother any mind, and she slid Jeremy into his arms.

"Just hold his head," she said. "You want to support his neck."

Chad beamed ear to ear. Andy took in her brother Brian, who was just inside the living room, refusing to sit on the loveseat beside their mother.

"Why did you run away, Laura?" Brian asked. He wore the same hurt expression that Laura often took on.

"I never ran away, Brian. Why would you think that?" she said. Andy watched the exchange between George and Sue. What had they done?

"You never called or anything, Laura," Chad said, and Laura looked between her brothers, just figuring out what Andy already had.

"Mom and Dad, did you tell Brian and Chad that I ran away?" she asked. Andy didn't miss how hurt she sounded.

"You know, sitting back and doing nothing, allowing someone to hurt my wife, doesn't work for me," he snapped. "I won't allow it. I expect you to treat my wife with respect. We may be in your house, and there's a lot of hurt between you; but if I had any other choice than to come here and ask you for something, Sue and George, well, Hell would freeze over. My boy Gabriel is sick, and without a bone marrow transplant, he'll die. I will not allow my son to die!"

"Who's Gabriel, Laura?" Brian asked, appearing confused.

"Gabriel is my son," she said, "and the reason I left. Mom and Dad asked me to leave when I got pregnant at fifteen. I kept Gabriel. I wouldn't give him up, and I did call after I had him. Do you remember that, Mom— what you said when I was in the hospital? You told me that if I wanted to come home, I had to give him up." She was so calm, and Andy was proud of her for holding it together.

"You threw Laura out? You lied!" Brian yelled at his mother. "How could you?"

"Brian, listen, it wasn't that easy, and what your sister did was …"

"Careful," Andy barked out, interrupting her before she could finish. "That's my wife you're talking about."

Sue firmed her lips and just shook her head.

"Andy, we need to finish this," Laura said, leaning toward Chad, who still held Jeremy.

"So Gabriel is your son, and you're the father?" George said. He wore an odd look, and Andy, although tired, was sharp enough to pick up on his meaning.

"I met Laura just over a year ago. Gabriel is not my biological son, but he is my son in every other way that matters," he said. George appeared to relax.

"Laura, who's your son's father?" Brian asked.

"It doesn't matter, Brian," she said, shaking her head.

"It does matter to me. Do I know him? Did he help you at all. Where is he in all this?"

Laura looked to Andy. He knew she didn't want to say anything, but if Andy had a sister, he'd have wanted to know who messed with her.

"His name is Tyler, and he turned his back on Laura," he said. "I just talked to him, got him tested. He's not in Laura or Gabriel's life, and he's not a match."

"Tyler Cassidy, from our church?" Brian fisted his hands. "Did you know?" he said to his father.

George and Sue exchanged an odd look, one of shared secrets. "Yes, we did," Sue said.

"I swear to God, I'm going to kill him. You've had him over for dinner with his family how many times?" Brian said. His anger had ramped up the energy in the room, and the babies were starting to fuss.

"Brian, let it go, please," Laura pleaded. "I never told you, so how did you know it was him?"

George glanced at his wife. "I'm an elder with the church. He was torn up over what he'd done. He came to me for forgiveness, for help, said he'd been led astray."

Andy didn't know what to say. He wondered what was wrong with these people. Brian still stood in the corner, his hands fisted. Andy was trying to get his head around the fact that these two parents had tossed their own daughter out into the cold; but had welcomed, into their home, the boy responsible for getting her pregnant. He wasn't even sure what scale of hypocrisy that put them on.

"Brian, maybe when you're a little older, you'll understand," Sue said. "Your father is an elder in the church. Tyler and his family are his flock. What your sister did, well, it embarrassed your father. We were just grateful it wasn't spoken of. This could have hurt all of us—"

"Stop this!" Laura shouted. "We're not here to talk about how I embarrassed you with your church. You made your choice. Fine. I have a life. I kept my son, and I'll do anything to make sure he stays alive. Please, he needs a bone marrow transplant from someone from this family. It has to be a perfect tissue match. I'm not a match. If I was, I wouldn't be here. Neither would my husband; but I'm begging you to get tested. If you're a match, then please, please be a donor to my son—our son!" She looked to Andy, and he could see she was shaking. "Could you honestly, in good conscience, live with yourself if Gabriel died and you could have saved his life?"

"Well, maybe this is God's way of punishing you. Have you ever thought of that?" Sue said.

For the first time ever, Andy wanted to slap this woman

for hurting his wife. He couldn't believe Sue was a mother. That she had given birth to Laura. She had ice in her veins. He wondered what the difference was between her and Caroline Friessen, his own mother, the ice queen who came from old money. His mother only cared about her position within the oldest Eastern blueblood families. This woman only cared about her position within their church.

He glanced at Laura, who had a tear running down her cheek as Chad handed the fussing baby back to her. Chad appeared embarrassed.

"Okay, that's enough, Sue," George said, gesturing quite sharply with his hand.

"I'll do it," Brian said, stepping into the middle of the room.

"Me, too," said Chad defiantly.

"Not without my permission, you won't. You're minors," Sue stated. Was she seriously going to push this?

"Laura, take Jeremy and wait for me in the truck," Andy said. Just one look told him she was frantic. "Trust me," he whispered, and he leaned in and kissed her.

It took her a moment and another breath until she stood up. Andy stood with her and could see she was shaking.

"Goodbye," Laura spit out, and she started for the door before stopping beside Brian, setting her hand on his arm. "Take care, Brian," she said. Then she glanced over at Chad, sitting in the same spot on the sofa, looking like a boy who'd had his favorite toy stomped on.

Andy just watched his wife, who scanned the room as if taking her last look. She left through the front door.

Chapter 24

Laura was halfway to the truck when the front door flew open.

"Laura!" Brian stepped out and hurried after her in his sneakers, laces dangling. He was seventeen now, she remembered, and he was tall and thin.

Laura pulled the blanket up over Jeremy's face as the rain splattered down a little harder. She had no hat, so her hair was getting wet, and her brother was soaked.

"Hey, Brian, it was so good to see you. I really missed you," she said.

The front door opened again, and Chad raced out. "Laura, don't leave again!" he said.

"We're getting soaked out here, you guys. Come sit in the truck," Laura said. She climbed in the front with Jeremy, and Brian opened the driver's door. Chad climbed in the back, slipping past the baby seat and sitting in the middle.

"Laura, why didn't you tell me what happened, that you were going to have a baby? I remember you were so upset, and then Mom said you left. She wouldn't let us talk about you. It was as if you'd done something horrible," Brian said.

"You had a baby, Laura?" Chad asked from the back seat.

She looked from one brother to the other and realized the hole in her heart that would never heal was from the pain of leaving her brothers; having no contact with them —*a bad influence.* Her mother's words rang through her mind again, making her feel worthless. It had taken her forever to hold her head up again.

"I had a baby. It happened. I didn't give him up. His name is Gabriel, and he's five. He's amazing and sweet," she said. Her heart ached, talking about him, worrying about how he was doing.

"You're married, Laura?" Brian asked. "You're barely twenty-one, and your husband is so much older than you. Is he good to you?" He couldn't hide his concern.

She smiled and nodded. "Andy's a good man, and he loves Gabriel as his own. I love him, and he looks after us." She smiled at her brothers. "So, tell me about you two. I can't believe how big you are! Brian, are you shaving?" She reached across and slid her hand over his chin.

"Brian has a girlfriend," Chad teased.

"A girlfriend, do I know her?" Laura was in awe of what she'd missed.

"She's a new girl, moved here with her family last year. She's nice. Her name is Donna. Mom doesn't like her, and she made Dad have a talk with me, saying I was getting too serious. You know how she is. Dad just does what she says." Brian reached over and rubbed his finger over Jeremy's hand, and he glowed when Jeremy wrapped his tiny hand around his finger. "That's so cool, what a grip he has."

The back door opened, and Andy leaned in. "Sorry to

break this up, but we have to go. Boys, your mom wants you in the house."

"Laura, how do I get a hold of you?" Brian asked. "Where are you living?"

"Yeah, Laura, I want to come with you," Chad added. "Don't leave us again, please. I want to help your son."

"Either of you have a cell phone?" Andy asked.

"I do." Brian pulled a small, slim phone from his back pocket.

"Give me your number. I'll text you with our address and phone number. You call Laura anytime; and if you two need anything, you call me," Andy said, keying in the phone number.

"Brian, Chad," George called from the front steps. "You come in now, you hear?"

Chad leaned forward and kissed Laura on the cheek before hopping out.

Brian touched her arm. "Don't worry, Laura. I'll help your son. After all, I'm his uncle," he said. Then he slid out, and she watched as both of her brothers went into the house. Her father lingered at the doorway for a second, just watching them, before he shut the door.

Chapter 25

The steam filled the bathroom, coating the mirror, as Laura lounged in the large bathtub of their hotel room for the night. The hot water soothed the ache from the tension she'd been holding on to for what felt like a lifetime. She could hear the twins jabbering away on the bed, where Andy had laid them down after bathing them. They were dressed only in diapers in the warm room.

There was a knock on the door, and Andy said in his deep voice, "Coming!" She wondered what he was doing when he poked his head in the bathroom, holding a baby in both arms. "That's dinner at the door," he said. "Don't fall asleep in there."

She didn't want to get out of the warm tub, but she was anxious to call Neil and Candy again so they could get another update on Gabriel. It was so hard to be this far away, and she was exhausted—not just physically. She felt as if she'd been in the fight of her life, battered and bruised, but she couldn't shake the sense that maybe she was stronger than she'd thought. She'd faced her parents without crying or falling apart. She'd held it together. Having Andy there with her had been a steel wall of support that kept her sane.

She listened to the rattle of a cart. There was another voice in the room, and then the door closed. Andy poked his head in again. "Dinner's here. Come out and eat."

Laura unstopped the tub and stepped out, drying herself off and slipping on one of the hotel robes before going into the room. It had one king-size bed and a playpen set up for the babies to sleep in.

Jeremy was making a lot of noise, and Andy was swaying with him. Chelsea was a perfect angel in his other arm. She had a big, bright smile on her face. She loved being with her daddy.

"I'll take him," Laura said, holding out her arms. Andy just shook his head, letting his gaze sweep over her with an appreciative glint.

"You look relaxed," he said. "You eat. He's just being fussy and demanding."

Laura took in the four plates with silver domes overtop. "What did you order?" she asked. She lifted the closest one and sniffed the steak and baked potatoes with broccoli, and the scent had her mouth watering, it smelled so good. Her stomach answered with a loud rumble even Andy could hear.

"There's salad, too," he said. "Chicken, as well. Dig in. There's lots." He set Chelsea in the playpen, Jeremy with her, and Laura took a plate and sat at the small table. Andy set a salad and a bottle of water in front of her. He lifted the cover from another plate and joined her. "I talked to Neil while you were in the bath."

Laura had just crammed a piece of steak in her mouth. She chewed and swallowed. "I thought you'd call after dinner."

He cracked open a beer and took a swallow, shaking his head. "Gabriel had a rough day, but he settled in with Neil and Candy. He apparently was able to play a game of Snakes and Ladders with Candy this afternoon."

"Well, that's good," she said, setting her fork down and leaning back.

Andy gestured with his hand and then picked up his own fork and knife, cutting into his steak. "Eat, Laura. Maybe I shouldn't have said anything until after you ate."

"I'm not a child, Andy." She picked up her fork again and took another bite, maybe just to prove a point.

"No, you're not a child. You're my wife, and I should have told you how proud I was of you today; the way you took on your parents. You held your head up, Laura, and you didn't let them knock you down."

She paused and watched her husband. He'd never said that to her before. For some reason, she had always wondered if he thought she was helpless.

"I guess I didn't know where I belonged as their daughter," she said. "I felt for so long like a nobody, and then I was just surviving. Then you came along and turned my world and way of thinking upside down. I've had to figure out who I am. It helped, having you there, knowing you wouldn't let them hurt me."

"You know who you are, Laura. You're my wife. You're a Friessen, and we don't allow anyone to walk all over us. No one will ever do that to you again."

She had never considered what Andy was saying. She'd always thought of herself as an extension of Andy, cared for by Andy. Now, as she thought about it, she realized he was right in a lot of ways. She may have been his wife and taken his name, but she was strong and capable. She had to be, to be married to him.

"So what do we do now, Andy, for Gabriel? My

brothers said they would help, but how do we get around my parents? I can't believe they would actually block this." She played it over in her mind again and again; how they'd just turned their backs so easily. Laura was having trouble believing she had actually grown up in that family. She wondered whether that feeling she'd had as a child, never fitting in, was because of all the superficial bullshit that came naturally to her parents. Being out of all that and away from them had helped her see clearly the face they put on for the community. A facade of togetherness, of family values. They saw themselves as pillars of the community, the upper middle class, well adjusted and normal, but that was a load of crap. They were greedy, dysfunctional, opportunists. She wondered how many other families were just as messed up. Maybe more than she realized. There was no such thing as picture perfect—it was all about who was better at hiding their secrets.

Andy tapped her plate with his knife. "Gabriel is going to be fine. Come on, Laura, eat."

She tasted the broccoli, which was a little soft, over-done and tasteless. "What did you say to my parents when I left?"

She watched Andy cut a big piece of meat, and he sighed. She wondered whether she was wearing him down, because he didn't cut her off the way he usually did. She could see his mind working, in an odd sort of way, as if considering what to say.

"Let me be clear about something: I don't like them," he said. "They hurt you. They're a miserable excuse for … I told them to name their price."

She wasn't sure what to say, and she could tell by the way he watched her that he didn't know how she'd react. Even Laura didn't know how to react to that. She glanced over at her babies cooing in the playpen. Then there was a knock on the hotel room door.

"Did you order something else?" she asked

Andy frowned and wiped his mouth with the napkin as he slid back his chair. "No, I didn't. Maybe they forgot something." He went to the door, and Laura stared at her plate, considering how it made her feel that Andy was willing to pay her parents off to save Gabriel. She wondered whether they were the type of people who could be bought.

"Hello, Laura."

Laura jumped and felt her face warm when her father stepped into their hotel room. She instinctively pulled at the front of her robe to make sure it was closed, that she was decent, and she looked right to Andy. She knocked her fork on the floor. She felt like an absolute klutz, as she bent down to pick it up, reminding herself that she wasn't a little girl. She was good, and she was decent. This man had no power over her.

Andy was right there when she stood up. He slid his hands possessively over her shoulders and held her still. "Your dad wants to talk about Gabriel," he said, and then he moved her beside him. With his arm around her, she could feel his strength, his power, protecting her. In that moment, she knew she could handle anything.

Chapter 26

Andy still couldn't believe George Parnell had knocked on their door. He was here alone with what appeared to be his hat in his hand.

"Dad, what are you doing here?" Laura asked. Andy could feel how she was fighting to hold every one of her emotions in check.

George gestured to Andy. "Your husband, here, made a very good point. I wasn't proud, Laura, about what happened; but your mother can be a difficult woman. I'm sure you understand this."

Andy couldn't believe this man was actually going to stand there and blame Laura's mother for his poor choices. For the fact that he hadn't figured out where his balls were. Andy had no respect for this man. In fact, he saw him as less than a little boy. He wondered what kind of role model he was for his sons.

Laura looked to Andy, and he could see she wanted to say something, but she frowned. Maybe she was having the same trouble he was.

"George, I frankly don't understand how any man

could allow a woman to make all the decisions, good or bad, and not have the backbone to stand up for what's right or wrong," Andy said. "You're supposed to be a pillar in the community, an elder in the church. Seriously, George, I wouldn't want you as a role model for my kids, let alone a mentor or anyone they could go to for advice."

The man appeared embarrassed—hell, "ashamed" was a better word for it. Laura set her hand on Andy's chest. "Let's hear him out," she said.

"Thank you, Laura. Your husband is a little hot under the collar," George said. Andy didn't miss the way Laura stiffened beside him.

"Well, Dad, my husband would walk through hell for me and our children. He'd do anything to protect us and keep us safe. He's an amazing man." She was holding on to Andy so tightly and looking up at him. "I know he loves us. I never thought it was possible to be cherished this way. I thank God every day for bringing him into my life."

Andy couldn't believe she'd said that. He was stunned by the passion and tears glistening in her eyes when she spoke about him. She was still watching him, although a little shyly now.

"Well, that's good. I'm glad you're being looked after," her father said. He cleared his throat uncomfortably. "I took to heart what you said, Andy, and I do have a conscience—whether you believe it or not. I'm not going to take money to help Gabriel. I'll get tested."

Andy hadn't expected this. George was all over the map. Although Andy knew there was a conscience somewhere in this man, he had thought it was buried so deeply that, in the end, the money would have won him over. "That's great," Andy said. "I'll call Doctor Siegel. He'll make arrangements here at the hospital for all of you to be tested."

Andy was so happy that he had already reached for his phone, about to make the call, when he noticed the way George winced and wiped his hand over his forehead.

"Andy, here's the thing. Only I'll be getting tested—not my wife or the boys," he said.

It was then that Andy noticed how George seemed to pull into himself, looking around the room in a self-conscious, worried kind of way. He hated that spineless behavior in men, yet here he was, face to face with a man who was all that. He just shook his head.

"Why, Dad?" Laura said. "Brian and Chad want to help. They'll hate you."

"Can't be helped. Your mother put her foot down. She won't allow them to be tested." He was shaking his head as if he had accepted that Sue's words were set in stone.

"Well, I think Chad and Brian might have other ideas, Dad—Mom doesn't need to know."

Andy was astonished that Laura had said exactly what he was thinking, but her dad was shaking his head.

"That's not how a marriage works, Laura. I thought you would have learned that much. That would be completely dishonest. Now, do you want my help or not?"

Andy squeezed Laura's shoulder before she said something else. He could feel her tenseness. "Of course. I'll make the call," Andy said, immediately dialing Bruce Siegel and passing along George's cell phone number. When he hung up, he thanked George, and by the time he had him out of the room and the door closed, Laura was fit to be tied.

"Andy, how could you thank him like that? He's just going along with my mother when we need everyone," she cried.

Andy made it across the room and pulled her into his arms. "Just stop and think about it, Laura. It only takes one. If your dad's a match—then we're good." He held her away from him, but she wouldn't look at him. She was still stuck, but he could see the moment she realized he was right.

"Fine, but what if he's not?" she asked. He wondered if she knew how far he'd really go.

"If he's not, then I'll get your brothers tested, both of them—with or without your parents' permission."

Laura studied him and tapped his shoulder. "Good. Now let's finish dinner and get some sleep, because I'd really like to leave early in the morning," she said.

Whatever this strong, assertive, together side of Laura was, Andy decided he liked it. Yes, he liked it a lot.

Chapter 27

They were halfway back to Columbia Falls when Andy's cell phone started ringing. "Yeah?" he said, watching Laura as she relaxed against the seat. She turned her head and raised an eyebrow, wondering who it was.

"Where are you?" Neil asked in a low voice that put Andy on edge.

"About three hours away, give or take. What's going on?"

Laura sat up a little straighter. "Is it Gabriel?"

Of course she was worried, and Andy was doing his best to hide his own freak-out from her.

"We've got a problem here," Neil said. Andy could hear talking in the background and then silence. "Tyler has been back twice to see Gabriel since you left. I got him out of the room the first time, but I was down getting coffee for Candy when he came back. Candy was cornered. She asked him to come back later, but he started talking to Gabriel. When I got back there, he was telling Gabriel some story about Laura when she was a teenager, before she had him."

"What?" Andy barked out.

Laura was instantly alert. She reached out and touched his arm. "Andy, who is it?" She was leaning forward, and he waved her off.

"It's Neil. Tyler has been there twice," he said. "Neil, is he still there?"

"Yeah, that's why I'm calling," Neil replied. "He came back with his mother."

Andy didn't have a clue what to do. He tapped the phone to his head and then set it to his ear. "Do whatever you can to keep them both away from Gabriel. Damn that kid. This is what I was afraid of. Did he say anything to Gabriel about who he is?"

"No, not yet, but I have a feeling it's only a matter of time."

"Where are they now?" Andy asked. He couldn't get there fast enough.

"Candy's talking to them in the hall just outside Gabriel's room. I already paged the doctor. Look, what do you want me to do? This is your call, but I wouldn't hesitate to get a lawyer on this now. You said you hadn't filed for legal guardianship. Well, you better get it rolling, especially with Gabriel this sick. I can get it started, find a really good lawyer to fast-track this."

"Look, I can't get there any faster, so do you think you could do me a favor and keep them occupied? Tell the doctor I don't want them anywhere around Gabriel; and yeah, find me a lawyer—someone good." He glanced over at Laura and didn't miss the way her eyes widened.

"On it. I'll call you." Neil hung up, and Andy was torn between driving all over the country, trying to save his son's life, or standing guard outside his door. He was just glad

Neil was there, because he'd do everything Andy would. That much he could count on.

"Andy, what's going on?" Laura asked sharply.

"You know how we've never talked about all the legalities of making Gabriel mine?"

She swallowed and took in what he was saying, and he wondered for a moment whether she truly understood what was at stake. "I just assumed, you know, when you married me …"

"Laura, Gabriel isn't legally mine. I have to adopt him. In the eyes of the court, I don't have legal guardianship until I do. Tyler is named as Gabriel's father on his birth certificate, isn't he?"

She set her hand over her mouth. It took a moment, but then her eyes widened as she understood the problem. "Yes, because he fathered Gabriel. Should I not have done that?"

Right about now, he wished she could have been one of those women who left the name blank. Deep down he didn't really mean that; even though it would have made things easier. "No, I'm just pissed off," he said. "That kid is taking advantage of the situation. He's shown up twice to see Gabriel since we left, and now he's back with his mother."

Laura's expression grew uneasy. She turned her head away to look out the window and then back to Andy, frowning. "Why would he do that? He wasn't interested in having anything to do with Gabriel. For God's sake, when I showed up at his door, he shut it in my face." She sighed. "Andy, could he interfere in Gabriel's life? If he really brought his mother, then she must know."

"I'll deal with them. Laura, we haven't had a chance, with everything that's happened, to sit down and talk about Gabriel becoming my son legally. Right now, we could have problems if Tyler decides he wants to have a voice in Gabriel's life."

"I'm sorry, Andy. I can't help thinking this is my fault. I just assumed, you know, that he's your son. We're married, and I never stopped to think about legal custody or anything. Andy, you're the only father he's ever had. No one could love him like you do. Yes, let's make this formal, whatever you have to do."

They only had to stop once to hurriedly feed the babies By the time they reached the hospital and pulled into the parking lot, the twins were both crying. Andy doubted they'd go back into a car seat anytime soon.

LAURA HAD to hurry to keep up with Andy. Although it did feel good to finally stretch her legs, she didn't like the fact that she almost had to jog to keep up. Andy had taken his son and the diaper bag, while Laura carried Chelsea, who was giving her a face, letting her know how displeased she was.

Andy pressed the elevator button a couple times and then reached for his phone, to send a text. Laura looked up and didn't miss the annoyed expression on his face.

"Who are you texting?" she asked, wondering if she sounded as out of breath as she felt.

"Neil, to let him know we're here."

The elevator door dinged.

"Andy, Laura," Neil said. They both turned to see him fast approaching. Tyler was with him, along with a middle-aged woman. She was short, compact, with reddish shoulder-length hair, a round face and big blue eyes. It took Laura a minute to recognize her, and Tyler and his mother exchanged a look that had her stomach sinking to her knees.

Neil looked none too happy. "Hey, guys. Glad you're back," he said. He was looking straight at Andy.

"Hello, Laura," Tyler added. "You remember my mom?"

"Yes, I do." She turned to Andy, willing him to do something, anything. "Andy, this is Tyler's mom, Nancy Cassidy."

It would have been impossible for Andy to miss how frazzled Laura was. He took in both Tyler and his mother. "I'm Andy Friessen, Laura's husband," he said.

"I'd say nice to meet you, but these are unusual circumstances," Nancy replied.

Laura didn't miss the uneasy way Nancy glanced toward her. There was something in her expression that set off alarm bells in Laura's head.

"To learn I have a grandson under these conditions, well … as you can understand, I was naturally upset," she said. "We always wondered what happened to you, Laura. I just don't understand how you could have kept this from me."

She firmed her lips, and Laura picked up on her disappointment. For the life of her, she didn't know what to say.

"Andy …" Laura looked to her husband. What could she say to the woman who had been her best friend's mother. The woman who had baked her cookies; at whose house she had sometimes spent the night?

"Nancy, I don't know what you've been told, but Laura was alone with Gabriel for years," Andy said. "She went to your son, and he shut the door in her face. That was a crappy thing to do, Tyler. You made it clear that you wanted Laura to go away and never bother you again.

Now you're here with your mother. Why?" Andy swayed with a fussing Jeremy.

Nancy gave Tyler one of her disapproving looks and shook her head. "You shut the door in her face?"

Tyler jammed his hands in his pockets, knowing he had just been caught in a lie. He shrugged. "I'm sorry."

Laura couldn't believe it now, but at one time she'd thought Tyler was everything. Had he ever grown up? "You're sorry?" she snapped. "My husband asked you a question, and I, too, want to know what your intentions are. Andy is Gabriel's father. A father is someone who loves his child, who protects him …"

"And that's what I'm trying to do for my son," Tyler interrupted with a stubbornness she hadn't seen before. "He's my son. In all fairness, Laura, you never gave me the chance to get to know him. You could have tried harder. You never let me know when he was born, if it was a boy or girl. After all these years, you could have said something."

She couldn't believe he was trying to turn this back on her. Neil appeared uncomfortable. For a moment, she wondered what he thought of her and what he'd been told about her over the past few hours. Obviously, it had been nothing good.

"I'd like you both to leave," Laura said, swallowing the dry lump stuck in her throat. "I seriously cannot believe you are putting this on me. I was the one who was forced out alone. You walked away. You don't get an opinion. You made your position clear, and I'm the one who had to struggle alone to feed him and to put a roof over his head. You don't get a say. You weren't there." Laura was getting really worked up, and Chelsea started fussing in her arms.

"I am his father!" Tyler shouted. "I have rights …"

"Whoa, whoa, just back up a second, here," Neil said, stepping in.

"Laura, go upstairs. Take Chelsea up. I'll be there in a minute," Andy said. By the dark look on his face, she realized he wasn't just quietly taking all this in. Tyler and his mother had stirred up the vengeful lion, but Laura had no intention of walking away.

"No," she said.

No? Damn his stubborn wife! Andy couldn't believe now was the time she'd picked to stand her ground.

"Hey, look, guys. This is not the time to get into anything," Neil said. "Tyler, you may believe you have rights, but I would think really long and hard about your intentions. There's a very sick little boy up there who's only ever known one father, and that's Andy. What exactly is going through your mind to bring this up while Gabriel is sick?" Neil waved across all of them with his hand. Of course, he was trying to be reasonable.

On the other hand, Andy wanted to hand his son over to Neil, grab Tyler, and drag him out of the hospital to knock some sense into him with his fists. He also wanted to sit him down and explain to him why it was in his best interest to walk away.

Laura wasn't moving. He could see the way she was working her jaw. She was furious and fighting back tears at the same time.

"Of course we're indebted to you, Andy, for caring for Gabriel, for being there for him," Nancy said, tucking her purse firmly under her arm. "But he is my grandson, and I can tell you that if I'd known, things would have been different."

Andy wasn't sure how to take that, but he sensed her meaning. She would have stripped away Laura's rights as a teenage mother and raised Gabriel herself. "There are no what-ifs here," he replied. "This is the way it is. Laura is my wife. Gabriel is my son."

"Not legally, he's not—and Tyler is not about to give up his rights," Nancy added.

Tyler, that punk-ass prick, had the gall to stand there and glare at Andy as if he was the one who had been wronged.

"So this is the way we're going to have to play it?" he snapped. "Nancy, Tyler, this is a pretty shitty thing to do when my kid is fighting for his life. I will be legally adopting Gabriel, and if I have to fight you in court to do it, I will."

"Andy," Neil added with warning. "You and Laura need to go up."

"I don't want to see either of you here again. If I do, I'm calling security!" Andy shouted. He set his hand around Laura and moved her to the elevator, jabbing the button again until the doors opened. They stepped inside, and before the doors slid closed, Andy watched his cousin speaking to Tyler and his mother. No one looked happy.

Chapter 28

Andy couldn't believe it when Doctor Siegel motioned him out of Gabriel's room. George Parnell was not a match. The results had just come in. Andy wanted to throw something, anything, across the room. He was just glad Laura had left with Candy to take the babies home. It gave him time to figure some things out with Neil, but he felt his world and his cozy family life crashing down around him.

"We're running out of time, Andy," Siegel said. "I just tested him after this last round of chemo. We don't need to do another round, but we've destroyed his immune system, so everyone needs to be gowned up. The babies can't come here anymore, either. This is crucial. We're working under a deadline, and there's no suitable match in the donor bank."

Neil was leaning against the wall, his arms crossed over his green sweater. He turned and looked at the activity down the hall, then back at Andy and the doctor.

Andy set his hands on the back of his head. "There was also Tyler's mother. Was she tested?" he asked. He looked to the doctor, who shook his head. "I guess I burned that bridge."

"Possibly, but I'll talk to her," Neil said, continuing to survey the hall. "If she's the loving, caring grandmother she insists she is; she'd jump in, wouldn't she?"

"That leaves Laura's mother and her brothers," Andy said.

"Make the calls. Get them all tested. We don't have time to sit around for much longer," Siegel said.

"What if none of them are a match, then what?" Andy asked. He didn't know how much more he could take before he lost it and started acting like the crazed madman he was beginning to feel he was.

"We're not there yet, so let's not go there, okay?" the doctor said. He took them both in for a long moment before he left them standing outside Gabriel's room. A nurse stepped out of the room shortly after, closing the door behind her and posting a sign that read, "Isolation."

"Gown up before you go in," she said. "Gowns are here. Put the soiled ones there. Wash your hands, too." She pointed to a cart outside the door with stacked gowns and a bin for the soiled ones.

"What's next—do you think?" Andy said, sagging against the wall and wiping his face. He was so tired. He hadn't had a decent night's sleep since this started. "I've worked a lot of deals in business and time crunched a lot of deadlines, but this … something comes at us every time we turn around."

Neil paced in front of Andy. "I got you a lawyer, one of the best in family law. She's on it now, but she did say that in order for you to adopt Gabriel, the legal father has to be deceased, given up his parental rights, or abandoned the child. Since the first two don't apply, she's working with the last. It'll be hard to prove, with Laura being so young, and

Tyler, too, when it happened. The judges could be very forgiving, considering Laura didn't push it and let Tyler know he had a son."

"You have to be kidding me!" Andy said. "He shut the door in her face. If that's not telling a chick to get lost and that you've abandoned them; I don't know what is."

"She knows. She's using that," Neil said.

"She … so this is a woman lawyer?" Andy said. He wasn't sure about that. For some reason, he'd always thought sharp lawyers were men.

"Yeah, I got you the best. It's quite a process. There's a social worker who does a home study, investigates your background. Gives you that nice, warm, tingly feeling, doesn't it?"

"Seriously, she told you all that?" Andy was a little surprised at all the hoops he would have to jump through.

"I knew most of this anyway. With Candy … you know we can't have kids. I've been checking out our options for a while." Neil looked away, as if he'd shared too much.

"I hope it works out for you, Neil. You'll make a great father to a kid who needs one." Andy pushed away from the wall. "So what's she going to do for us in the meantime —since it's not likely adoption is going to happen overnight?"

"No, it's not. In the meantime, we have to save Gabriel's life. I'll talk to Tyler's mom—you get Laura's brothers and mother."

Andy watched as Neil walked away. He turned into the lounge, sifting through the numbers on his cell phone, stopping on a missed text from Laura's brother.

How's my nephew? How's my sister?

Andy texted back: Gabriel's not good. Need your help.

He waited a minute, and the phone pinged.

Whatever you need, I'll do it. Say hi to Laura.

Andy messaged back and then phoned the doctor, who answered on the first ring. "Can you arrange another test at the same hospital for two more from Laura's family?"

"Absolutely, just make sure the parents have given their signed consent for the boys," the doctor said.

"All right," Andy replied, knowing he should feel guilty for his omission. Whatever repercussions came from this, he'd deal with them at another time. If Brian was a match, he'd move heaven and earth to make sure they got the sample.

Chapter 29

"They have a match? Are you kidding me?" Laura was walking in circles in her kitchen, Candy gesturing excitedly in the background. She had a light baby blanket tossed over her shoulder and was burping Jeremy. "Oh my God, Andy!"

His deep chuckle on the other end of the phone was torture. She wished he could be here so she could throw her arms around his shoulders, hugging him, and kissing him, and just breathing him in.

"You did it, Andy," she said. She was getting all choked up. She hadn't pictured this moment—what it would feel like. Everything had happened so fast, and even though this was what they wanted, it still felt as if it had come out of left field "So who's the match?"

"It's Brian," Andy replied.

Laura glanced out the kitchen window looking at the pickup pulling up in front of the house. She looked at the counter and took in the sight of the coffee pot, still filled with day-old coffee. "I'm stunned. I can't believe Mom came around, Andy. I never would have believed it. How did you talk her into it? I mean, my mother is one of the hardest, most opinionated, stubborn people I've met. She'd rather go to the grave with a mistake than ever admit she was wrong," she said. When Andy didn't answer, Laura had an awful feeling she wouldn't like what she was about to hear. "Andy?"

He sighed on the other end. "She doesn't know. Just let me handle it," he said. He sounded frustrated.

"How's Gabriel doing?" she asked, still thinking of what to do—wondering if he was right and that she should just let him handle it. She also couldn't help but wonder how he thought he was going to get around her mother.

"He's getting through it. He's one tough little kid. I can see how he's fighting to hold it together, and he's doing better than most grownups—but it's rough. I just keep telling him it's okay, it's almost over, and he just nods. I'm not about to let him down. You understand?"

"I love you, Andy. Whatever you have to do, you do it," she said, and she hoped he understood. He was going against her mother, and that wasn't good. To Laura, Sue Parnell was a stranger; and for the first time, Laura understood who her true family was: Andy, Gabriel, and the twins. They were her family, and they were all she'd dreamed of having, in an odd sort of way—just not like this.

She held the disconnected phone and realized Candy was at the door, talking to someone. She set the phone down and strode out until she spotted Kim.

"Hi, Kim, how are you?" she asked. For the first time, she was genuinely happy to see her. Maybe she'd finally gotten a handle on that jealous streak of hers.

Kim seemed a little surprised by her reaction but then offered a bright smile in return.

"Kim was just asking how Gabriel's doing," Candy said. "Maybe you want to share?"

Candy had such a lovely voice, and she was becoming more comfortable with the babies every day. She was a true friend, and she was family, too. If Laura had a sister, she would've wanted her to be like Candy.

"We have a donor match. Andy just called," Laura said. Her voice held some hesitation, and she wondered if either woman had picked it up. She'd love to have a word with Candy alone; and she wondered if Candy could see her guarded expression.

"That's wonderful, Laura," Kim said. "That's such good news. You must be relieved, as I understand it, that was the hardest part for you."

"Yeah, I am … now we just need to hope the transplant works and that my little boy stays in remission—cancer free."

It was such a long road to recovery, but she felt they were standing at a crossroads now; and Andy would do everything in his power to see that they kept going. God help whoever might stand in their way. This was maybe the first time Laura had ever been glad her husband was who he was.

"Well, my prayers are with you. I just wanted to stop by and see if there was anything I could do. Ladystar is doing well, though. She's developed quite the friendship with my twelve-year-old Paint." Kim glanced over at Jeremy, propped on Candy's shoulder. "Hey there, you cutie-pie." She rubbed his back, and Laura didn't miss the longing look in her eyes. It was very sad and lonely, and then she stepped back. "Well, I should get going." She pulled open the door.

"Kim, I don't know what Andy and I would have done

if you hadn't offered to look after Ladystar. I know he'll be happy to hear she's doing well," Laura said.

Kim just nodded and stepped out, closing the door.

"You don't have to be worried about her, you know," Candy said as she wandered into the living room. Laura followed.

"I know," she replied. "It just took me a while to figure it out. Andy is …" She stopped and sighed, glancing away; but by the way Candy watched her with a knowing look— Laura knew she understood what she was trying to say. "He's so difficult, arrogant, and strong willed. I didn't think he'd ever let me in. He's so proud, and I know he'll never give in. I knew he cared for us, but to know he loves me and that he's trying … I can be so insecure and stupid sometimes. When I met Kim, she was together, and strong, and capable. She could handle anything Andy could, and I felt incompetent."

"She's not as together as you think," Candy said. "None of us are, Laura. We all have our fears and things that hold us back. You just have to understand that some are better at hiding it. I can also guarantee that Kim may envy you and feel mighty self-conscious around you, as well."

Well, that had her stumped. Laura had never believed anyone could envy her.

"You can see it in her eyes," Candy said. "You have a husband who loves you so much he'd do anything, including walking through fire—for you and your children. You have three amazing kids, and I didn't miss the longing when she looked at Jeremy. You have a beautiful home, this land; and you don't have to worry anymore about how to keep a roof over your head and pay the bills." Candy gave her an odd look and shrugged.

Laura swallowed. She wondered how much Candy knew of her background.

"I've been close to where you were," Candy said. "When I met Neil, I had a lot of pride—so I understand. Sometimes we don't know how to count our blessings."

Laura considered what Candy was saying. She had never stopped to appreciate all the good things in her life. "I guess with what happened to Gabriel, I didn't even realize I've always seen the negative in things—wondering whether they could get any worse. Instead, I should be thankful Gabriel's alive, that he has Andy—who loves him as if he were his own, and he's going to beat this."

"Good girl. You just hold on to that," Candy said, and Jeremy picked that moment to spit up.

"Oh, sorry! Here, let me get him cleaned up." Laura went to reach for him.

"No, I've got him. Besides, he's not as scary as I thought he'd be. I'm kind of having fun. Neil was right— just don't tell him, please. I don't want his head to swell any more than it already has," Candy said as she cuddled Jeremy. As she took him down the hall to his room, she whispered all kinds of things that had him cooing. Laura hoped that Candy and Neil would be lucky enough to find a child to love.

Chapter 30

It had come to the point that Andy could make the trips back and forth to the hospital in his sleep. After a week of holding his child, worrying, getting through each day, and fighting his bone-tired weariness; he had to remind himself there was a light at the end of the tunnel. There was a lot riding on this transplant, and he shoved all the gigantic hurdles that kept flooding his mind away. He didn't have the luxury of allowing himself to get dragged down into any of these details.

He knew he'd done some things that could land him in a lot of hot water. Brian had texted him after the bone marrow aspiration was taken from his hip, and Andy had made sure a driver was waiting to take him home after the procedure. It had been tricky, with all the lying and sneaking around—but Sue Parnell wasn't about to offer consent. Brian, after several long conversations with Andy, had convinced him that telling his dad was the same as inviting his mother in to put a stop to everything. So Andy had gone along with a seventeen-year-old who was determined to play the hero.

Since Doctor Siegel had made all the arrangements and Andy had ensured the medical costs were covered—no one had questioned the fact that Brian was a minor. Five days ago, Andy had looked Doctor Siegel in the eye when he asked if Brian was over eighteen, and he'd said yes. Of course, the doctor had been ecstatic—reminding Andy that good things happen, and that the ideal age for a transplant donor was between eighteen and twenty-four. He had also reminded Andy that over seventy percent of those waiting for a transplant never got the right match.

Andy wasn't proud of what he'd done, but he also wasn't about to hire a lawyer and wait for a court date over this. The legal process could be dragged out until it was too late. Even though Brian had said he would do anything, Andy somehow didn't think Brian understood the emotional shit he might have had to go through in court, further dividing his family. This way was better, easier, so why did he feel as if something bad was coming his way?

"You ready?" Neil slid his hand over Andy's shoulder from where he stood outside Gabriel's room, taking a minute and just watching the hall as if waiting for something he couldn't explain.

"Wish they'd hurry up and get this done," he said, feeling a little choked up. He blew out a breath roughly. "How's he doing in there?"

"Laura's reading to him. He's doing better than you." Neil grabbed a spot right beside him and leaned against the wall.

"I can't shake this feeling, Neil, that something's going to go wrong; like maybe I'm paying for every bad thing I've done."

"Hey, don't start looking for trouble. You did what you had to. Don't start getting all noble on me now." He tapped Andy on the arm. "Hey, look, there's the doctor."

Doctor Siegel was wearing light green scrubs and was approaching fast. He stopped at the nurses' station, grabbed a chart and flipped through it. Whatever he was reading, he seemed satisfied, and he continued over to Andy. "We're ready to get going," he said. "They'll bring him down, and one of you can come down with him; but not into where we do the procedure. It won't take long, so take a breath, and go get some coffee. You've come this far, and this is a good match." He patted Andy's shoulder.

Andy glanced over at Neil when the doctor walked away. "Okay, maybe you're right," he said. "I'm just tired, so I see problems around every corner."

"Listen," Neil said. "Tonight, I'll stay with Gabriel. You go home with Laura and get a good night's sleep. You've been here day and night since Gabriel got sick."

Right about now, Andy wished he could think as clearly as Neil. He could use some sleep, but he didn't want to leave Gabriel, and he'd seen the way it tore Laura up; having to leave him every night. "All right, you're on," he said. "If Gabriel is doing good after the transplant, I'll go home tonight. Thanks, Neil."

Two gowned-up orderlies and a nurse went into Gabriel's room. Andy and Neil both grabbed a gown and followed. Laura was sitting on the bed with Gabriel, and she locked eyes with Andy.

"Okay, Mister Gabriel, we're going to take you down," one of the nurses said. She had a grandmotherly way about her, and she was the nurse Gabriel really liked.

Laura slid off the bed. "Can I go down with him?"

"You can walk down with him, but you can't stay while we do the procedure," the nurse said.

For the first time, Andy didn't want to be the one walking him down. He needed to be watching, standing guard to make sure this whole thing happened, and then he could relax. He couldn't tell Laura, so he stepped to the foot of the bed and touched Gabriel's leg. "Hey, bud, we're almost there. They're going to take you down and make you all better, just like we talked about."

"So then I can come home?" Gabriel said in a hopeful voice.

"Then you can come home," Andy said. He'd make sure of it.

Andy waited with Neil in Gabriel's room after they'd taken his boy down, and he let out a breath he'd didn't know he'd been holding, releasing the knots in his back and shoulders. Neil phoned Candy, and Andy noticed the big grin plastered on his face as he spoke to his wife.

When he hung up, he was still grinning. "The twins are good," Neil said. "Candy is having so much fun with them. I knew she'd come around. She was so nervous and worried about breaking them at first. She'd never held a baby."

Andy tried to look happy for Neil, but he couldn't shake the worry that was still hanging over him. He knew that until Gabriel was wheeled back into this room, he'd continue to worry. "She's getting comfortable around the babies? That's great. Are you planning on adopting?"

"We've talked about it, and I'm checking out our options. There's a really long wait list to adopt, and I always wanted a child that was mine. I'm just happy Candy is having fun with your babies, that she's getting comfortable. I was starting to worry I'd never convince her she'd be a great mother, but I knew she would. She was terrified of children. It took me a while to realize how scared she was, but she was afraid because she had never held a baby or a child," Neil said with humor. Just then, Laura wandered in through the open door.

"Are they doing the procedure?" Andy asked from the stuffed vinyl chair he'd become well acquainted with.

"Yeah, they're doing it now. They said it wouldn't be long."

Andy held out his hand to Laura, and she went right to him, sliding onto his lap, resting her head on his shoulder.

"Oh God, I think I could go to sleep here," she said.

Andy set his arms around her, running his hand up her legs and over her butt in the skinny blue jeans that made her look so incredibly hot. He rested his head on top of hers and took in Neil watching them.

"I told you to stop worrying," Neil said. "You're home free. Why don't I go and grab coffee for everyone?"

There was some activity outside the room, a doctor and a couple of nurses talking, and Andy couldn't help but notice the way they glanced into the room. An older man who Andy guessed was in his fifties, of average shape and height, with light hair and a mustache, tapped on the door. He had on a white doctor's coat, a shirt, and a tie.

"Mister Friessen?" He stepped into the room, and he had that look of authority about him that had Andy's heart hammering. The man glanced from Neil to Andy.

Laura started to sit up, but Andy kept his hands around her, holding her on his lap. "Yes, I'm Andy Friessen."

"I'm Chief Burns. Could I have a word with you, please?" He wasn't asking, he was ordering, and anyone listening could have figured that much out.

"Did something happen with Gabriel?" Laura stammered, and Andy could feel her shaking.

"No, your son is fine." He stepped further into the room and then gestured to the door. "We should speak outside, or can we talk here?" He gestured to Neil.

"This is my cousin Neil. Whatever you have to say, you can say it in front of him."

The man nodded and closed the door. "Very well. We seem to have a problem. Did you know the donor is a minor?" the doctor said rather brusquely.

Of course he knew. He just couldn't believe they'd found out. How? Andy's adrenaline shot up, but he somehow managed to hold it together. He didn't move, just stared at the doctor and then slowly looked over to Neil, who stood with his arms crossed, wearing the best damn poker face ever.

He just prayed Laura wouldn't say anything. He squeezed her hand, and when she looked at him, he took in all the worry and fear—his worst nightmare, mirrored in her eyes.

"From what I understand, the donor is your brother, Missus Friessen," Chief Burns said. At least he was being polite to Laura.

He watched her swallow, and she started to shake her head. Andy linked his fingers with hers.

"Look, he's almost eighteen," Laura blurted out. "Just let it go."

"Laura," Andy said in warning, hoping she understood.

"Andy, what now? Did they finish the procedure?" She was frantic. Hell, even he was a mess, but he wasn't about to lose it, not now. One of them needed a clear head.

The doctor crossed his arms and looked from one to the other. "Do you have any idea what kind of position you've put this hospital in, the lawsuit you've opened us up to? No, I stopped it."

"Fuck!" Andy yelled as he stood up, holding Laura and then setting her down. "Why would you stop it?"

Neil just shut his eyes, holding his chin between his thumb and forefinger and shaking his head.

They had almost been safe. They'd met the deadline.

Everything had fallen into place—everything except the awful feeling that had been poking him over and over. He'd ignored it, and it was now glaring at him from across the room, biting them in the ass.

"Seriously, Mister Friessen? You were complicit in obtaining an illegal sample that can't be used without parental consent, which we do not have, and Doctor Siegel … well, I'll be talking with him. If due diligence hadn't been done by one of the clerks in record keeping—"

"A clerk in this hospital is responsible for this?" Andy was furious, and the chief didn't appear to be amused by his outburst. Andy looked to Neil and back at the chief. "You're telling me some person in your clerical department decided to play junior detective and, what, they get off on fucking up kids' lives?"

"This isn't about a clerk. This is about what you did, and Doctor Siegel could be in serious trouble for ordering the procedure done," Chief Burns snapped.

Laura was frantic. Neil hadn't moved or said anything since the bomb had been dropped on them.

"So what now? You have a perfectly good sample that will save Gabriel's life," Neil said, gesturing as if this was a no-brainer. It was, with Andy, anyway.

"What we have is a sample we can't use. It will stay frozen, and Gabriel will be brought back up to this room to wait until there's a match. He's one little boy; and I'm sorry, but I will not jeopardize this hospital and the patients in it," Chief Burns said. He didn't speak in a booming voice, but it was direct and deep, and Andy knew the man couldn't be swayed. He was the law here, and he was what stood between saving Gabriel's life and ending it. "One more thing, Mister Friessen; you are not the legal guardian for Gabriel, which has also been brought to my attention. You married the lad's mother, but he's not your son, and you don't have the authority to make medical decisions on his behalf."

This was going from bad to worse.

"What? Andy is his father," Laura said. "He married me because of Gabriel. He loves him, he loves us … Andy, what are we going to do?"

"Laura, stop it," Andy said, taking her arm and holding her to his side.

"I'm not completely insensitive, so there will be a meeting this afternoon in the hospital boardroom, and I've invited all relevant parties to end this dispute," Chief Burns said. "I suggest, in the meantime, you figure out a way to resolve this peaceably with the people involved." He waited a minute and took them all in before pulling open the door and leaving.

All Andy could think of was that there was right, and there was wrong—and what they were doing was so very wrong.

Chapter 31

What could Andy do when people he didn't know were standing between him and his child's wellbeing?

He had gone home, showered, and changed, taking a minute to look over his babies, who were sleeping peacefully in their crib. These were his babies, and, legally, he had a voice. No one could tell him that he couldn't make decisions on their behalf. His lungs hurt, as if glass was scraping his insides every time he took a breath. He couldn't comprehend that others could decide what was best for Gabriel.

Maybe picking up and moving to Montana, to a county that didn't know him and didn't know the Friessen name, hadn't been such a brilliant idea after all. He wondered, as he slid his hand over Jeremy and then Chelsea, who was sleeping in the other crib, how a parent could stand in the way of someone trying to help another child.

"You all right?" Candy was in the doorway behind him. She had smoky dark eyes, and long, dark hair; a sensual look about her that was different from that of the doe-eyed bride he'd first met when Neil had been about to marry her. Then, she'd been terrified of her own shadow, afraid of all the babies and children running around.

"I never thanked you for jumping on a plane with my cousin and coming out to help us," Andy said, starting out of the bedroom. Candy stepped back to allow him to pass and followed him into the living room. She was a very attractive woman, wearing a tight brown sweater and blue jeans—his cousin's rock on her finger.

"Of course we'd come. Neil got your call; and being married to a Friessen, you learn fast enough. It was a little intimidating at first—how you all have each other's backs. I'm sorry about what happened. Neil called and told me. He said Gabriel is back in his room, resting, and Laura is with him."

Andy nodded, swallowing and pushing up the sleeves of his light blue knit sweater.

"What time is this meeting?" Candy asked.

"Soon." Andy glanced at his watch. For the life of him, he hadn't figured out what to do. Of course, his lawyer was ready to file a motion and an emergency hearing, but he really didn't want to go that route unless he had to. "This is the first time in my life that I feel everything is stacked against us," he said. He leaned on the window and looked out at the barren grass and debris he still needed to deal with.

"Well, you're emotionally involved. It's hard to be objective from where you are." Candy moved into his line of sight. She crossed her arms, and he wondered what it was about her that made her seem so innocent, and experienced all at the same time.

"So, from your perspective, how would you handle

this?" he asked. Right about now, any advice would be welcome if it would get Gabriel his transplant.

"Well, you have a mother who is strong willed and determined, and her husband has no voice. She has to make all the decisions and needs to have that control to feel wanted and needed."

"That makes no sense. How could Laura's mother be that unreasonable?"

"It makes perfect sense, Andy. Every woman wants to know a man can make a decision and will have her back, will respect her. When she has to be the strong one, it takes over. You need to let Laura's mother know you have her back. You need to speak with her alone, to be respectful, is my guess. And Tyler, well, I can only assume this is all about his guilt and what he did to Laura. You need to talk to him, get him to understand, let him see how Gabriel is better off with you."

"Well, that's easier said than done," Andy said. He pushed away from the window and took in Candy, a woman he barely knew. "Thank you, Candy."

He started to the door, lifting his coat from the chair and sliding it on, and then headed outside.

"Where's Andy?" Laura said. She was sweating as she paced outside the board room. Doctor Siegel had already appeared, leveled his frosty gaze at her, and then disappeared into the chief's office.

Neil was staring at his phone, thumbing through the screen, and he glanced up when someone walked by. "He'll be here. Don't worry."

"Neil, what are we going to do?" She touched her

damp forehead and then jumped when a familiar voice called out behind her.

"Hello, Laura," her mother said. She was wearing a mousy brown coat, her cropped hair framing her oval face. She looked determined. Behind her strode George, his hands in his pockets. Laura was surprised to see her brother with them, and his face was flushed rosy pink. He mouthed to her with a pained, wide-eyed look, "I'm sorry."

"Laura," said Tyler as he came from the other way, his mother beside him. Both of them carried their coats and were dressed in light sweaters, everyone looking neat and tidy.

Everyone converged and stopped just outside the boardroom, looking at each other. It was Tyler's mother who took in Laura's mother and said, "Sue, nice to see you again. Unusual circumstances."

Neil was watching everyone, and he carefully pocketed his phone. Laura fisted her damp hands at her sides.

"Mom, I can't believe you would actually put a stop to this. My son needs that transplant to survive. I knew you hated me, but I didn't realize you hated me so much that you would hurt my innocent little boy, who has done nothing to you!"

The look Sue leveled on Laura was frosty, chilling. If Laura hadn't been so close to losing it, she would have taken a step back.

Neil moved forward. "My name is Neil Friessen. I'm Laura's husband's cousin. My wife and I flew out to help once we heard Gabriel was so sick, and we'll stay here to support Laura and Andy as their family. You must be Laura's father, George." Neil actually reached out and took Sue's hand, which startled her, before reaching for her father's. "Brian, Laura has told me a lot about you. Tyler, Nancy, it's good that everyone could meet."

"So where is your so-called husband, Laura, who is responsible for all this? He left you to clean it up, didn't he?" Sue said. The way she spoke felt like a slap to Laura.

"I'm right here, Sue," Andy said, stepping beside Laura and sliding his arm around her. "I'm sorry. I've been living day and night at the hospital. I slipped home to shower."

No one said anything. Neil cleared his throat.

The chief's door opened, and the older man who had arranged all this stepped out, Doctor Siegel with him. "Folks, is everyone here?" He took in all of them as if he was counting.

Doctor Siegel started into the empty boardroom, flicking the light on and taking a seat at the end of the table. Everyone else filed in. Laura sat beside Andy, Neil on her other side. Tyler and his mother took a spot beside the doctor, while Brian, George, and Sue took up the other end of the table. The chief closed the door and stood at the head, taking them all in.

"I've scheduled this meeting to resolve some things. First, just so everyone is clear; the hospital, and Doctor Siegel were in no way aware that Brian was underage."

"This was entirely on me," Andy said, putting it out there in a strong, clear voice that let everyone know he wasn't ashamed of what he'd done. "This is my kid. I love him more than my next breath, and I'd sell my own soul to give Gabriel a chance to live. It's what a father does for his child. A father will sacrifice everything for his kid and will put his kid before his own ego, before everything. All I'm asking, begging, is that each of you give this five-year-old boy a chance to live. He's sweet, and he loves his baby brother and sister, and his pony. He just needs a chance to grow up, to date, to learn to drive and get his first car, to fall in love and get married …"

Laura was stunned by the passion in Andy's voice as he pleaded.

"But you're not his father," Nancy said. "You may have married Laura, but Tyler is his father. I'm his grandmother. Sue, you're his grandmother. How do you have any rights here at all?"

Laura could sense all the egos and ruffled feathers in that moment, which could turn this meeting into a free-for-all. That wouldn't be good for Gabriel.

"Fine, Nancy, so what is your agenda here?" Andy said. "What exactly are you trying to do to help Gabriel?" He leaned onto the table and waited for her to respond.

She opened her mouth to speak and then looked at Tyler. "Well, we wouldn't be lying and sneaking around, stealing a minor's bone marrow."

"So you're more interested in letting Gabriel die?" Andy was so blunt that his words cut into Laura like a dull knife, digging into her heart. She didn't know if she could take it.

"Of course not. We don't want him to die, but there's a better way to do this," she said. When Laura looked, she realized Tyler was watching her in a way she couldn't understand.

"Folks, this isn't getting us anywhere," the chief said.

"No, it's not, but I think Sue and Nancy have some things they need to say," Andy said, gesturing to both of them.

Sue was quiet at the end of the table, taking in Nancy and then Tyler.

"Folks, just so you understand, there is a deadline that happens with the type of leukemia Gabriel has. He's already been through two courses of chemotherapy to destroy the cancer cells, and with it his immune system. He has mouth sores, diarrhea, and what he manages to eat—he can't keep down. His little body is in agony, and he's fighting to stay alive. His hair is falling out and will continue to, which is minor, but he's handling it," Doctor Siegel said.

"In order to survive, he needs a bone marrow transplant, but it can't be from anyone. He needs a perfect tissue match that you can only get from family. Donor banks can rarely provide that, and only seventy percent of patients who need a bone marrow transplant get the perfect match. It's not as easy as you think. There's no match for Gabriel in the donor bank, and there's only one match we've discovered for Gabriel. That is Brian," Doctor Siegel said. He was poised in his seat, taking every one of them in. "I'm not saying what was done was right, by Brian or Andy, who were both working together to make this happen—but I can't believe that anyone in this room would willingly prevent this little boy from getting better."

Sue and George were quiet at the end of the table, and Brian slouched in the chair between them. "I may only be seventeen, but, Mom, if you don't allow my bone marrow to be used to save Gabriel, I'll never forgive you. I will go to court, and I'll ask that a judge take away your rights, as a parent, to make any decisions for me," Brian said.

Andy would have kicked Brian if he was closer, because he could see Sue digging her heels in even more. This was definitely not the way to handle her.

"Sue, give my grandson the damn marrow. George, for the love of God, do something!" Nancy said. Tyler said nothing, as he was still watching Laura.

"Sue, could I have a word with you alone?" Andy said in a reasonable voice that had her taking a second look.

"What are you doing?" Laura asked, and he leaned

down and whispered to her, "Just trust me, okay?" She took in his haunted look, which touched a part of her that made her unable to say no.

"Please, Sue," he added in a voice Laura recognized as the one that could convince her to do anything.

Laura watched as her mother took Andy in and then nodded as he stepped around behind her, slid out her chair, and guided her out of the room.

When Laura glanced over at Neil, he winked at her, leaned in, and said, "Don't worry. Your husband's got this."

Chapter 32

"Thanks for speaking with me, Sue. I wanted to apologize to you. I'm not proud of what I did, and I could have handled the situation better," Andy said as they walked down the hall and he guided her into the elevator.

She was holding her purse tightly under her arm, and he knew she wasn't going to make this easy. She was carrying a lot of hurt, and he could see the pride she carried as if it were the only measure of her self-identity. The elevator dinged, and the door slid open. Andy set his hand on the door to hold it open and gestured for her to go first.

"You know, Laura is the one who taught me all about love. She and I have come a long way. I love her, and I love Gabriel. I would do anything to protect them. When I met her, she had no control in her life, and it just about killed me to see her hurting," he said.

"You like to bully people—make things happen because you have money and you're powerful," Sue said.

As they walked, he noticed only slight glances here and there from her.

"I'm sorry. That's not my intention. I just don't want Laura or my children to ever have to worry about anything. I like to take care of all the details so they have a roof over their head and nothing bad can touch them. I'm overprotective of my family. Can you blame me?"

This time, she did look his way. She took him in. "Laura married well. I can see you love her."

Andy stopped at the closed hospital room door. He pushed the door open and reached for two gowns on the cart. "Here, put this on."

She took the gown and said, "Where are we going?"

"I want you to meet your grandson," Andy said. He watched the woman, noting the shock that appeared on her face and the moment of indecision. Andy wondered if she'd refuse as he held the door wider. He knew she had to see the little boy lying in the bed, tubes running out of him.

She took one step and then another into the room; and Andy let the door close behind them. He slid his gown on over his jacket and stepped around to the other side of the bed; and Gabriel rustled and opened his eyes. His face was pale, and hair had fallen out onto his pillow.

"Andy, where were you?" he asked.

"I had to go home to take a shower, but I'm back now."

"Where's Mommy?" he asked. He sounded so scared and tired.

"She'll be back soon. Don't worry, bud. I'm going to make sure everything's okay." Andy didn't miss the way Sue watched Gabriel, and he hoped she could see the resemblance to Laura—and to her. It was there in his expression, the shape of his face.

Gabriel glanced up at Sue and asked, "Are you a nurse?"

She appeared startled, so Andy added, "No, this is a friend of mine. Her name is Sue."

Gabriel actually smiled at her and said, "Nice to meet you, Sue." Damn, he was so polite. If Sue's heart didn't melt from his little boy's gentle spirit and kind soul, then Andy didn't know what it would take.

"Gabriel, it's nice to meet you, too," Sue said, and then she turned and hurried out the door.

"I'll be right back, bud," Andy said. He hurried after her and found her struggling to rip off the gown. Gently, Andy set his hands over hers. "It's okay, Sue. Let me help," he said, and he helped her out of the gown. He touched her shoulder, and when she looked up at him, she had tears in her eyes.

"I'm not a monster, Andy."

"I know you're not a monster." He watched her as she set a trembling hand to her mouth.

"You wanted me to see him like that," she said accusingly.

"Yes, I did, but not to hurt you. In all fairness, it's about having all the information. You needed to meet Gabriel. There shouldn't be anyone sneaking behind your back, but that little boy is your grandson, and he deserves a chance, Sue."

She was nodding and struggling not to cry. "Okay, you can use the marrow," she said, and Andy did something he thought he'd ever do: He hugged Laura's mother.

Chapter 33

"Laura, wait up," Tyler called out as she stepped out of the conference room with every intention of checking on her son.

She stopped just before the elevator and slowly turned, her stomach sinking at the thought of talking to Tyler alone. She knew Andy wouldn't like it, not one bit. Tyler hurried toward her, tall and lanky, clean cut. He looked good, wearing blue jeans and a green sweater, a bright shade that really brought out his eyes. He stopped and sighed, giving her one of the smiles that used to turn her good sense upside down and have her melting like a lovestruck fool. Now she found herself seeing how different he was from Andy. He just didn't measure up.

He went to reach for her arm, but she stepped back and shook her head.

He raised his hands. "Sorry, my mistake."

"What do you want, Tyler?" she asked, and she wondered if all the hurt she still carried echoed in her voice.

"Hey, I just thought maybe we could talk. I am

Gabriel's father. We have a child together, and there are probably some decisions we should be discussing for our son."

Laura crossed her arms, wanting to tap her foot in disbelief. Seriously, what was with this guy? "Let me get this straight: I was fifteen, and you were how much older than me?"

At least he had the good grace to blush.

"You got me pregnant. I wasn't alone, but, you see, I couldn't walk away, because it was my body. You shut the door in my face right after my parents threw me out; and if I remember correctly, after you had your fun with me, you treated me as if I was nothing—worse than nothing. You hurt me, Tyler."

"Hey, I'm not proud of what I did, but we both made mistakes." He was getting louder when he spoke and was starting to sound too familiar, as if he thought she'd wronged him.

"Did you know I had to quit school? I don't have a high school diploma. I lived in a shelter, I worked as a maid, I cleaned toilets, I scrubbed floors—anything I could to keep a roof over my son's head, to feed him. I did it alone, Tyler, and where were you? Oh, yeah, having fun, going to my parents' for dinner, dating, going to college. You don't have a say when it comes to my son." She jabbed her finger at him.

"I'm sorry, Laura. If I could go back to that day, I'd like to think it would be different," he said, and it seemed as if he truly believed that.

"Really, Tyler, you're so naïve. That's wishful thinking. You know what I am thankful for? I'm thankful for my husband, Andy, because he is Gabriel's father. He may not have fathered him, but he's his dad, and he's who Gabriel cries for when he's scared. He's who has been here every night with Gabriel, with no sleep, holding him while he pukes and cries and screams. He chases the nightmares away. He's the one walking through hell for Gabriel. No, you are not his father. Walk away, Tyler, because if you decide to push this, you'll have a fight that you don't want. You don't want to mess with my husband!"

"Are you threatening me?" he snarled. He took a step toward her and reached for her arm, and the next thing she knew, Andy was behind her.

"Get the fuck away from my wife! You touch her again, I swear to God I'll kill you," Andy said, grabbing Tyler and slamming him against the wall. There was yelling, and Neil was there, pulling him off. The anger shooting from Andy's hardened stare at Tyler should have sent him running. Andy was trouble when he wanted to be, but when provoked, when something of his was threatened, she knew he could be downright dangerous.

"Calm down, Andy," Neil murmured. He was there, and so were the doctors. George was pulling Tyler away, and Brian was there as well, squeezing his fists. He, too, looked as if he was ready to take a piece out of Tyler.

Nancy stood off to the side, watching all of them, and she said in a low and quiet voice, "Laura, I'm sorry. I didn't stop and realize how hard it was for you."

Laura was shaking when Neil let Andy go. He grabbed Laura and pulled her to him, and when she heard someone behind her clear their voice, she looked back and noticed her mother watching her, and then Andy. Her gaze drifted to Andy's arms around her, and she nodded as if satisfied with something. "Your husband already knows, but you have my permission to do the transplant," she said.

Chapter 34

Andy kept glancing into the backseat at Gabriel, belted into his high-back booster, with a fleece blanket over him. Laura was in the passenger seat, and she smiled every time Andy looked their way. To hear the news that he was in remission, that the transplant had been a success, had left Andy choked up, and he'd had to fight to blink back the tears. Neil had been there, slapping him on the back and gripping his shoulder as Andy pressed his fist to his mouth. Laura had burst into tears and slid into his arms, burying her face into his chest as she fisted his T-shirt. Andy had kissed her ear, her head, and finally buried his face in her short hair, unable to fight the tears. He'd wiped his face, embarrassed, and Laura hadn't let go. It was emotional; and the happiest moment of his life, and he knew he'd remember it forever.

Now, as he drove the long, winding gravel road to their new home, it felt as if this was the first time again—as if they were getting a chance to go back in time. The grass was greener, the snow was gone, and it seemed as if they'd missed an entire season. It took him a second to notice the dozens of vehicles in the distance, parked around his sprawling rancher, and there was a moment of confusion as he wondered whether he had the right place. "Laura, what's with all the vehicles?"

She scooted forward in her seat, the leather rustling, setting her hand on her window. "I don't know," she said. She looked at him and back out the window as Andy pulled up and parked behind a fancy Dodge Ram pickup. It seemed the vehicles were all pickups—and then he saw Neil, all smiles, moving their way with Candy behind him. Each held one of the twins.

Andy slid out of the truck. "What's going on here?" he asked. He spotted Kim, wearing blue jeans, hair nicely styled, with a bright gold top and a jean jacket.

"Your neighbor, here, said you were never properly welcomed. It's a welcome home party for Gabriel and to welcome you to the community!" Neil said. "I know there are a few people here who want to meet you."

Kim waved at Andy but went to Laura, hugging her and sliding her arm around her. "I hope you don't mind, but all your neighbors put together a welcome home potluck. There are a lot of folks here who were rooting for you, and for Gabriel; and they want to meet you."

Andy reached for Jeremy, who was babbling away in Neil's arms. He kissed him and then handed him back. "He's grown so much," he said. "God, I missed these two." He reached out and rubbed his finger under Chelsea's chin, tickling her. It was the first time he saw her face light up, and she let out a little giggle.

"Let me grab Gabriel," Andy said as he opened the back door. Gabriel already had his seat belt undone, and Andy lifted him out, tucking the blanket around him. His red hat covered his bald head. "There's a party here for you!" he said, and he kissed him on the cheek and moved beside Laura, who was standing with Kim.

"Well, why don't we say hi to everyone, and then I'm going to get you tucked into bed?" she said.

"I want to party!" Gabriel added. Of course, Laura looked into the house at all the people they could see through the windows.

"Come on, Laura. Let me introduce you to some folks," Kim said. She slid her hand around Laura's elbow and led her to the house, giving her only a second to look back at Andy with a helpless expression. Neil and Candy hung back.

"Did you have to let them in the house?" Andy asked.

Candy appeared worried for a second. "Well, Andy, she's your neighbor, and they brought food, lots of food. They seem like nice people."

"They do, Andy. Just come inside to meet everyone. I think you'll be glad you did. I think Gabriel would like to meet some of the younger kids, too. There are a few his age who he'll be going to school with. Besides, Gabriel's doctor is here, too."

When Andy glanced down at Gabriel, the boy wore a hopeful expression. After weeks of being sick and taking treatments, coming home to this welcome for him and their family—well, it had to be good for him. "Okay," Andy said. "Just no cake, no sugar, and you're not running around."

When Andy stepped inside, Bruce Siegel appeared.

"Andy, you have to be happy to be home," he said. He set his hand on Gabriel's leg. "Hey, Gabriel, how does it feel to be back?"

"Good," Gabriel said, smiling and taking in all the people in the house.

Neil appeared a second later. "Hey, Gabriel, let me

steal you from your dad. Your babies are being spoiled by all your neighbors." He scooped him up, and they disappeared around the corner, leaving Andy with Doctor Siegel.

There was awkwardness, and he wondered why the doctor was here after what had passed between them.

"I'm surprised you're here," Andy said, and the doctor gave him an odd look.

"Why wouldn't I be? You're still my neighbor. Kim's my friend. She called and insisted, so of course I had to come," he added. From the way he watched Kim from across the room, Andy wondered if there was something between them.

"I'd do it again, you know," Andy said. He wondered what the man would say to that. Maybe he'd leave, but Andy was too damn tired to care. He was playing nice, after all the crow he'd had to swallow to make things right with the hospital and Laura's mother—and then there was Tyler.

"Yeah, I know you would. I can't fault you for what you did. Just don't ever pull that with me again." He reached out his hand to shake Andy's. It was strong, solid, a man Andy had to respect. After all, he'd saved Gabriel's life.

Bruce patted his shoulder, and Andy moved on. After meeting a dozen neighbors, shaking hands, he spotted Laura, who was across the living room, speaking with a light-haired man wearing a black leather coat. He spotted Jeremy being cuddled by an older woman—and there was Candy, who looked as if she wasn't about to relinquish Chelsea any time soon.

Andy slid his arm around Laura, wondering who the charming man was. He had bright blue eyes and an easy smile. He was a little too dashing, young, and interested in his wife, and Andy had to suppress that possessive growl inside him, as the man was making him downright territorial.

"Andy Friessen," he said to the man, who flashed the same smile over to him and reached out a hand. Of course, he accepted and squeezed hard. The man didn't flinch but seemed to find humor in what he did.

"This is Pastor Johnson," Laura indicated.

"Jamie, please. We're informal here. I was just telling your wife how excited we were to hear about the nice young family who moved here. We wanted to welcome you. It's nice to see someone living out here in this place. It's been empty a long time. Your wife tells me you're going to raise cattle."

Laura was looking at him mischievously.

"Yeah, that's the plan, which was kind of put on hold, but yes, as soon as I can make arrangements."

"Well, if you need any help or anything, let me know. I grew up on a ranch in the Midwest. I was riding before I could walk. My father, his father—well, you can say ranching was in their blood."

Andy shook his hand again. "Thank you. I'll keep that in mind. If you'll excuse us, I'm going to borrow my wife for a minute."

The young pastor, who looked more like a biker wannabe, moved away to a couple of older gray-haired ladies who were all smiles and laughter as soon as he joined them.

"So that's the local minister, huh?" Andy had to admit he didn't fit his idea of what a minister should be.

"Yeah, kind of surprised me. He doesn't talk like one I've ever met. He didn't try to convert me."

"Interesting" was all Andy could think to say. The doorbell rang, and Neil called out to him and waved. "Guess more of the community is here," he said. He kissed

Laura and then left her, making his way across the room. He slowed when he realized Neil wasn't smiling.

"Tyler's here," his cousin said in a low voice. "He's waiting outside."

Andy glanced back at Laura, who was speaking with another neighbor he hadn't met yet. "Where's Gabriel?"

"Bathroom, with Candy. He's fine," Neil added. "Do you want me to come?"

"Yeah, see what the hell he wants now." Andy pushed the door open, really digging into each step. He was pissed and angry, and he couldn't believe this punk-ass kid had the nerve to show up here, at his home, where friends were throwing them a welcoming party.

"Tyler," he bit out. He could feel Neil beside him as he took in Tyler, with his light face, his awkwardness, and the way he stood with his hand jammed into his pocket.

"I'm sorry to just show up here, but I wanted to give you this," he said. He was holding out a manila envelope. For what felt like an eternity, Andy just stared at it. Whatever was in it couldn't be good. He kept his arms crossed, and it was Neil who reached over and snatched the envelope from Tyler's grasp.

"So what is this? You're hell bent on fucking up my kid's life even more? You're not satisfied that he's happy, that he has two parents who love him and whom he loves—"

"Andy," Neil said, stopping him before he could say anymore. "You need to see this." He set the legal paper in front of him, and Andy blinked and read it again, because his brain didn't register what it was saying. *Termination of Parental Rights.* He wasn't sure he'd read it right. He looked up at Tyler, who appeared ready to weep.

"I wish things could be different, but I signed that

because I do love him. I wish I could go back and change things. I wish I could be a part of his life."

"I don't know what to say," Andy added, feeling like a bastard for jumping down Tyler's throat. He reached out his hand, and Tyler stared for a second. Maybe he was worried Andy was going to hurt him, but then he pulled his hand from his pocket, stuck it out, and gave Andy the weakest, limpest handshake before quickly pulling away.

"Just promise me you'll take care of my son. If you could send pictures, let me know how he's doing … maybe one day you could tell him about me, when he's older," he said. Then he shuffled away, stepping off the porch, and Andy called out to him.

"Tyler, thank you," he said. The kid waved as he hurried back to a green minivan, where his mother was waiting behind the wheel, and they pulled away.

"You didn't promise him you'd send him photos or update him," Neil said.

"No, I didn't."

"Hmm." Neil set his hand on his shoulder. "So what are you going to do?"

"Finalize the adoption," Andy said, waving the paper in the air, "so no one can ever question my parental authority again." Andy slid the paper back in the envelope. "Let's go join the party."

Two days later, Andy was organizing his office after saying goodbye to Neil and Candy. He'd sent his lawyer the signed termination of rights, and she was moving the adoption process along. Tomorrow, he'd finally meet the man about some cattle.

Laura called out from the kitchen, "Andy, dinner is ready!"

"Coming, just need to put something away." He patted the envelope he'd been looking for when they first arrived, the one that contained Aida's tape, the evidence of his mother trying to get rid of Laura. He'd stumbled across it with Neil after the party, when he'd been poking around in some boxes, and he'd since made a copy.

He slid open his desk drawer and pulled out a locked box, opening it and shoving the envelope inside along with a silver bank key and instructions to a safety deposit box at the bank in town. There was one thing Andy knew: He would always make sure his family was safe.

Turn the page for a sneak peek of
THE PRICE TO LOVE the next book in THE FRIESSENS: A NEW BEGINNING
Available in print, eBook and audio

The Price to Love

A 2015 Readers' Favorite Award Winner

She could give him everything except the one thing he wanted—A child.

—Lorhainne Eckhart, is courageous to write a story with a "good guy" who is so despicable in his behavior. That does not ruin the story, though; if anything, it adds realism and volume to the plot."

SUSAN

—Any book that has me wanting to cry and yell at the characters this much...a story that holds me to it so much I don't want to put it down....THAT is a good book!

LORNA

—"I don't know if I should love him or hate him, but I couldn't put it down"

—A. CUSTOMER

—"I loved this emotional roller coaster."

—MIMI BARBOUR, NEW YORK TIMES BESTSELLING AUTHOR

—"I was pulled in on the first page and could not put it down until I got to the last page. I love when a writer tells the story about a complete family."

—SUSAN, REVIEWER

She could give him everything except the one thing he wanted—A child.

Candy knows that her husband wants a baby, but she can't give him one. When Neil pays for a surrogate and moves her into their home, he tells her not to worry, but she suddenly feels as if she's on the outside looking in.

Then, one day, she meets a little girl who steals her heart, a little girl with a damaged, scarred soul filled with the kind of despair and hopelessness that should never be in the innocent eyes of a child. But neither Neil nor his family understand her need to help.

As their marriage hangs on brink of disaster Candy is forced to make a choice between her husband and helping this child.

Chapter 1

There was something about the breeze, the way it drifted across the bay in harmony with the waves as they slapped against the sandy shore. It was stirring, peaceful, and powerful being this close to the salty spray of the ocean, and it helped clear her head. Candy Friessen rolled her shoulders and breathed in the fresh morning air as she walked beside Sable, her smoky gray Azteca and best friend … though she could never tell her husband that she considered her horse her closest confidant!

Neil Friessen would never understand, because the fact was that he believed her world should rotate around him, not in an arrogant, conceited way but more a way that showed her devotion to him and their family. Neil was so committed to family—his family, his picture-perfect idea of how his family should look. Candy knew he believed they were as close as two human beings could be, and he thought of her as his best friend. He was her husband, her lover, and, at times, her confidant, but there were still some painful parts of herself that she couldn't share with him.

Those fears and dark thoughts she could only share with Sable.

Neil wanted to be a father more than anything. It was his dream, his burning desire, to have a family—but it was the one thing Candy couldn't give him; a child, *his* child. That had been taken from her at her darkest hour, when she had been left barren after an emergency hysterectomy was performed to save her life. She had been so young! She knew it wasn't fair, but she'd learned to live with this agonizing, hollow feeling deep inside; though it was an emptiness she couldn't share with her husband, only Sable, who understood the deepest parts of her soul, the things she couldn't say to anyone.

She also knew there were still options if they wanted to have a family. One door had closed while another had opened. The doctors, and their family, all meaning well, had said so—but Candy knew her husband well enough to realize that his dream of having a child of his own was the one thing that would always come between them. Oh, he loved her. She knew that, as he wouldn't have married her once she'd given him the opportunity to walk away. She wondered, though, if there were times he regretted what he'd done. Maybe she was reading too much into it, but this was what she did on her mornings alone with Sable as they walked side by side down their sandy white Cancun beach.

When she tossed around the idea of what was next in their journey, it always came down to one thing—how much she loved Neil. To stop loving him would be like suffocating herself. She couldn't do it. She loved her magnetic, charming, and powerful husband—and he was *hers*. Every time he was with her, he touched her, talked to her, took over her thoughts and senses. His hold over her was unsettling, now that she was away from him and had the space to think, but she had to admit there was something addictive about him giving her all his attention. He knew how to look after himself, too, which added to the attraction and the dynamics between them. Of course, his confidence and inner strength made her believe he would always take care of everything. He made her feel safe, loved, and cared for … as if she were in a bubble that could burst at any moment.

Neil Friessen was everything to her, and the man still had the ability to take her breath away. She just wished she could be as confident in their love, especially considering Neil was oblivious to the fact that any warm and breathing woman would have given him a second look, doing everything she could to get closer to him. It bothered Candy, though she knew this was a sign of a lack of faith on her part. Neil was smart and loving, always holding her hand and waking her with a wild, burning passion every morning, and she loved all of that about him, but she still couldn't tell him about this feeling she had, this building confusion, as if something was about to change everything —all because of what he was proposing now—a surrogate. He had mentioned it the night before, out of the blue, but just the idea of another woman carrying his child was too much to bear. Candy shut her eyes at the thought of another woman stepping in to do something she couldn't. It left her feeling impossibly lonely.

Sable nudged her shoulder as they walked side by side down their beach until the resort, in full construction, came into view. She stumbled and slowed at the chaos of the pounding, the constant buzz of power tools, creaky scaffolding, and workers. She stopped by the fence that was the gateway to her private beach—and to Neil's multimillion-dollar resort. He was erecting it where her house had once been, the property owned by her father, which he had left to her when he died. What had once been there had been swept away by a storm the previous year.

It had been her land, though she had lost it to her creditors. Neil had coveted that land for years, but after buying and paying for it, he'd given it back to her. It had been a gift of love, and she hadn't been able to deny her husband his dream. The beachfront resort he was now building had once been an obstacle between them, but she trusted him to do what was best for the land because of how much she loved him.

Candy looped the lead rope around Sable's neck and slid the halter around his muzzle and over his nose before tying it at the post. He was starting to skitter from the noise, and their connection had been lost. She held him steady when a sudden bang had her heart racing and Sable spooking. "It's all right, Sable," she murmured. "Let's turn around and head back home and away from this noise."

It was loud and chaotic, a huge project that provided jobs to a community that desperately needed them. She understood that, but it was hard to let go of what had once been. The tide had turned, changing her life in ways she could never have imagined. She had once fought this sort of change, but her love for Neil had helped her overcome her fears.

"Candy!" she heard her husband call out, and she picked up their pace, starting back down the beach until she spotted him.

He was dressed so neat and tidy, with dress pants and a white shirt. His dark hair was neatly groomed, and he walked purposefully toward her. "I've been looking everywhere for you," he said. "Why didn't you tell me you were taking your horse out and coming down here to the beach?"

She kept walking toward him. It was always his eyes,

their intensity, that reached out to her and pulled her to him. She could never look away—even though being with Neil, being his wife, sometimes made her feel as if she were drowning.

"Next time, let me know if you're coming down here," he said. He glanced over her shoulder at the fence and the workers on the other side; there was something in his expression that had her looking back.

"Neil, I always came down here before," she said. What was going on? At times, Neil could be overbearing and overprotective; it stoked her temper, but there was something about the way he watched the workers that bothered her.

"I don't want you down here alone anymore. Can't that just be the end of it, Candy? Why do you have to question everything?" Neil said, sounding annoyed.

This was so unlike him, and she found herself watching him the way she would Sable, trying to figure out what was going on. He sighed and shook his head, gesturing toward the construction.

"I didn't mean to say it like that," he said. "I just can't explain it. There're a lot of riffraff around right now, workers coming in from all around Mexico, and I haven't had the chance to get to know any of them yet. I don't want to be worrying about you right now, and I don't want something to happen to you. Do you understand?" He stepped closer to her, and Sable nudged him as he put his hands on her shoulders. His eyes slid down, and she knew he was taking in her very short white shorts, white tank top, and sneakers. He lifted her long, dark hair over her shoulders and tucked strands behind her ear. For a moment in time, it was just them. "Tell me you'll listen to me," he said, "just this once."

How could she deny him when he looked at her the

way he did, as if she was the only thing that existed for him in that moment?

"You know how much I love this; the beach, the ocean, spending time with Sable," she said. "I need to do this every morning. It's who I am, Neil, and you agreed to keep this part of the beach ours."

He touched her cheek and rubbed the pad of his thumb over her lips as he tilted his head closer, really taking her in. It was distracting, he had to know. "I promise I'll come down with you every day," he said. "It's just not safe right now. It won't always be like this, Candy. I promise."

She could smell his minty breath. She could feel his warmth even though his lips hadn't touched hers yet.

He took a deep breath and said, "I got a call from a possible surrogate."

She couldn't help the way her body instantly stiffened.

Thankfully, Neil didn't appear to have noticed, as his hand slipped away and dropped to his side. He stepped back, looking impossibly happy. "She'd like to meet us in an hour."

She felt as if she were being sucked into a vortex. Her ears rang as she watched joy fill his expression. She hadn't even had time to digest the idea, and now he was barreling right ahead as if he wanted no further discussion. No matter how hard she tried, she couldn't see eye to eye with him on this. Why did he always have to move so quickly on his ideas?

Maybe her feelings were showing, as his smile faded and his expression became serious. "What's wrong?" he asked.

"I just don't understand why you feel a surrogate is the only answer. I mean, you haven't even considered adoption, and there's an orphanage so close by. There're a lot of children, young children, who need parents, Neil."

"Candy, you know how I feel," he said. "I want a baby, a child of my own. You already know that with an international adoption, there would be a waitlist, interviews, red tape. We're Americans, Candy. As difficult as it would be to adopt in the U.S, we wouldn't even know what we were getting into here. We'd be old by the time a baby became available. No, this is better; less mess, fewer problems."

She wanted to finish for him, to say what she knew he was really thinking. He wanted a child with his blood, his genes, one that was biologically his. If there was one thing about Neil Friessen, it was that when he wanted something, he never allowed anything to stand in his way.

"I see. So your mind is made up?" She swallowed the lump that had formed in her throat.

"Candy, we've discussed this. We've already decided. I know you want a baby. I saw how much you loved looking after the babies when we stayed in Montana at Andy and Laura's. You have no idea how happy I was to see how comfortable you were with Chelsea. You loved holding her. I could see how much you wanted a baby. Let me give that to you."

"Neil, I loved caring for Chelsea and Jeremy. Your cousin's twins are adorable babies. But I'm also a realist. I think we need to talk about other ways. You only mentioned surrogacy last night! I need time to digest this, to discuss all the aspects of it with you. I need to be comfortable with this entire process."

She could feel him pull back even though he hadn't moved one step. He looked away and sighed. She knew he felt disappointed, annoyed, frustrated—the same way he felt whenever he couldn't get her to think his way. She was smart enough to let him believe he'd convinced her, and she remembered what his mother had once said: *The Friessen men are so strong, both physically and emotionally, that , at times, it would have been easy to lose herself.*

"Candy, why do you have to argue and overanalyze everything when a good thing comes along?" he said. "Sometimes you just have to go with it. Please don't fight this, baby. Let's talk to her. We'll figure it out."

He went to reach for the lead rope to take Sable from her, but she held tight and started walking. "So where are we meeting this woman?" she asked, swallowing again. This feeling, whatever it was, had stirred up all her vulnerabilities; the ones she thought she'd put to rest long ago.

"Here," he said. "She's coming to the house."

Every nerve in Candy's body zinged, and she stopped suddenly. Sable picked up on her shock, prancing and raising his head. Neil reached for the rope before Candy could gather herself and took it from her hand.

"Let's go," he said. "You have enough time to get cleaned up and put on something nice." He started walking away with her horse. "Candy, come on," he called out over his shoulder.

Candy watched as Neil walked away. He was her husband, who had taken over everything and in turn had provided her with a life any woman would give her right arm for. For some reason that she couldn't explain, their marriage was snowballing into something else, and she realized she was quickly losing who she was—losing her sense of self and her ability to stand on her own two feet. It bothered her because he was making it so easy for her to slip into that role of being cared for, allowing him to handle everything. The problem was, that if something ever happened to Neil and she found herself alone, she would be more vulnerable than ever.

Hours later, Marcus is called to a crime scene. The body of one of the escaped prisoners has been discovered deep in the woods, and the scene has already been lit up, with three prison guards standing over the body, along with the sheriff and deputy from the county over and a tracker with his dogs. A story has been neatly put together, and the group at the scene tries to send Marcus on his way.

Yet one prisoner is still missing. Marcus is told no investigation is necessary, that he should sign off on the case and walk away. But nothing adds up. The problem is that dead men can't talk, and Marcus can't shake the feeling that the story he's being told is a coverup for something far more sinister.

The Hunted, Chapter 1

T he sound of crickets punctuated the quiet neighborhood. Darkness had settled in, but Marcus needed a minute, as he leaned against the large porch beam, before he could lock up for the night and feel that all was okay in his part of the world. He lifted his hand in a wave to his brother Owen and his wife, Tessa, as they drove away in her small compact. Again, he took in the neighbors' houses. Next door, the lights were off and all seemed quiet.

Ryan and Jenny were already inside their house across the road, and the outside light was now off. Marcus waited for that feeling he got every night before locking up, an assurance that it would be okay for him to lay his head down and go to sleep. He counted heads, making sure everyone was okay, listening to the sounds inside his house, the fussing of Cameron, who was doing his nightly protest against going to sleep.

The screen door squeaked open behind him, and Marcus turned to see his dad step out, wearing blue jeans and a black t-shirt. He heard his mom and Reine talking inside. His dad nodded to him and headed over.

"Your mom is finishing up in the kitchen with Reine and Eva," Raymond said. "That boy of yours is just like you. You always fought your mom and argued every night about how you weren't tired, but a second later you'd be out cold. You didn't know how to stop."

Marcus turned to look back at the street. He was still trying to understand his dad. He leaned against the post on the porch, breathing in the warm summer night. The smell told him tomorrow would be another hot day.

"You were rather quiet tonight," Raymond said. "Everything okay?"

What was he supposed to say? This feeling had come out of nowhere. He couldn't remember ever having felt so unsettled, and he didn't have a clue what had caused it—family, life, something else?

"Just one of those days, you know," Marcus said, unable to find words to explain it.

His dad only nodded. It wasn't lost on Marcus that his dad had been forced to stick around Livingston because his mom had refused to leave her children and grandkids. His dad had a way of seeing everything. Marcus had figured that much out, but a stranger wouldn't have been able to tell, as Raymond never let his gaze linger too long.

Now he did, narrowing his eyes, peering out into the darkness. The stars were out, and a few streetlights were on. "Always the sheriff, looking out to make sure everyone is tucked in, safe," he said. "Expecting trouble?"

Marcus looked over to his dad. Inside, the house phone was ringing, and a second later, it was answered. "You know something I don't?" he said. The sarcasm dripped.

His dad only shrugged. Marcus heard footsteps and pushed away from the post just as the screen door squeaked again, and Reine stepped out, her dark hair pulled back, wearing a peach sundress, barefoot.

"Marcus, it's for you," she said. "It's Therese." She held out the cordless phone.

Marcus didn't look over to his dad, who he knew was watching him in the way only Raymond O'Connell could. Marcus took the portable phone. "Thanks, Reine," he said, then waited as she walked back in the house. He put the phone to his ear, glancing only once to his dad, knowing his deputy called only if there was something he needed to handle. "What's up, Therese?"

"Sorry to call so late, Sheriff, but I have a message from the warden from Montana State. Two prisoners have escaped, and all he said was that they could be headed this way. I was about to call him back…" There was static on the line. His deputy was cutting in and out, as if she were driving.

"Hey, Therese, you're cutting out. You said two prisoners escaped from Montana State?" He was already walking back into the house and taking the stairs two at a time. Upstairs, Charlotte was reading to his son, whom he thought he heard jumping on his bed. Marcus was in his bedroom now, yanking open the closet door and opening the gun safe to retrieve his .357 SIG.

"Sorry, Sheriff," Therese said. "I'm about twenty minutes away, and the cell service is like shit out here. Picked up the message on the way. All it said was that two prisoners escaped. The warden is…"

"Kellogg," Marcus cut in, fastening the holstered gun to the waistband of his jeans. As he closed up the gun safe, he pictured a man he'd met only a few times.

"I missed that part of the message," Therese said. "I'll give him a call and let you know what he says."

Marcus glanced to the open door. His wife now stood

in the doorway. "No, Therese, I've got it," he said. "I'll have Charlotte check the message, and I'll give the warden a call."

She said nothing, and he noted her hesitation.

"Anything else?" he said, realizing it had come out rather short.

"No, that was all," Therese said. "You sure, Sheriff? I don't mind making the call. It may be nothing."

"Or it may be a lot," he said. "No, I've got this one." Then he hung up and held the phone out to Charlotte, taking in her wide eyes.

"What's going on, Marcus?"

He reached for his badge. "Prison break or something along those lines. Therese just called, said the warden at Montana State left a message. Two prisoners. I need you to get his number and play that message for me."

She was already nodding and dialing the office. Something about his wife handling phones and dispatching again settled him in ways he couldn't explain. She scribbled down the number on a pad of paper on the dresser just as his two-year-old son came running in, all smiles, appearing nowhere near ready to go to sleep.

Marcus reached for him and gave him a toss in the air, then held him and kissed his cheek. "Hey, you. Giving your mom a hard time? You're supposed to be asleep."

"Not tired."

"Yeah, well, you will be soon. Go get a book and get in bed."

"Here, Marcus, the number," Charlotte said. "The message is kind of garbled, but yes, it's something about two prisoners escaping."

He put Cameron down after kissing him again and reached for the paper and the phone, shaking his head over his rambunctious son.

Charlotte shook her head. "He's going to be the end of me. You know he argues every night about how he isn't tired?" She pulled her arms over her faded green t-shirt, her dark hair pulled up in a ponytail. "You're heading out, aren't you?"

"Yeah, after I call the warden," he said. "I don't like this."

There it was, that smile of hers he loved. She leaned in the doorway, glancing once over her shoulder down the hall to where their son's bedroom was as he dialed the phone.

"Montana State, warden's office." The voice was muffled, and Marcus had to really listen past the rough twang.

"This is Sheriff O'Connell, from Livingston. Is the warden there? I've got a message from him about a prison escape."

He heard a rustle on the other end, then a clunk. Evidently, whoever had answered barely knew how to use a phone. "Yeah, yeah," the person said, then yelled out, "Warden! Call for you from that Sheriff O'Connell."

Marcus reached for his wallet and stuffed it in his back pocket, then reached for his duty belt. Charlotte didn't look away, gesturing for an explanation, but Marcus only shook his head. There was another rustle on the phone.

"Sheriff? Warden Kellogg here." The man had a deep voice. "Afraid two prisoners escaped. Was discovered only a short time ago by one of the guards. We're in lockdown now. Just finished a count and are interrogating some prisoners. We know two got out for sure, but how, we have no idea. They likely had help from inside. I suspect they could be headed your way. These men are dangerous, both of them. I've already contacted state officials, as well, along with the other sheriffs in the area. An order has already been issued: Shoot to kill."

Marcus angled his head, looking right at Charlotte. He wasn't sure he'd heard the warden correctly. "You can't be serious," he said. "Who authorized that order? With all due respect, Warden, capturing the prisoners is the first priority."

"Sheriff O'Connell, these prisoners are a danger to the community," the warden said. "They will slit your throat and kill you without a second thought. If you want to dance around them and be the nice guy, do it on your own time and not at the detriment of the good people of Montana. You see them, you shoot them, because these two will do anything and everything to avoid capture. Killing, maiming, looting, burning. You want the details of what they'd do to your wife and sisters, everyone in your family, everyone you care about? If you want to argue with me about bringing them in alive, you can do it, but I don't want these two getting anywhere near innocent people. I've already reached out to Judge Harris, and photos of the prisoners have been sent to you."

Marcus didn't have a clue who these two prisoners were or what they'd done, but that sick feeling was back in his stomach with the image of the horror the warden had painted. Damn, what kind of evil had the two men done?

On the other end, the warden was talking to someone else. Then he addressed Marcus again. "Anything else, Sheriff? If not, I suggest you get your ass out there and start looking. Stan has faxed over the photos, and emails have gone out statewide."

Something about Warden Kellogg had always unsettled Marcus, but he couldn't put his finger on what it was. "Yeah, you said they could be headed my way. Why is that?

They have family, friends, contacts here? I need all that information."

"Everything about both prisoners has been sent to you. One has a girlfriend, I understand, outside Livingston, and a brother up toward Billings. If that's all, Sheriff, I've got a fucking mess to handle here. You have any questions, get in touch with Sheriff Lester up in Stillwater County. He's got more on them, and he's been on this since word went out. And, Sheriff O'Connell? A word of advice. I understand you may want to give these men a second chance, but sometimes we're all better off if a criminal is six feet under. You understand?"

Yeah, he understood, but a knot twisted in his stomach as he looked over to his wife. He wondered if this explained the sick feeling he had or the cold sweat that had broken out up his spine. "Understood," he said. "I'll start looking." Then he hung up and tossed the phone on the bed.

"What is it, Marcus?"

Marcus counted the extra clips in his duty belt, then walked over to his wife and ran his hand over her shoulder. "Warden says the prisoners had help from the inside to get out. Says they're dangerous. Photos have been faxed and emailed. Can you access those? I'm going to ask Mom and Dad to stay until I get back," he said. It was just a feeling he had, the need to keep his family together. "See if you can pull up the prisoners' files, too. Warden said they've been sent. I want to know everything about them: who they are, what they did, and exactly how dangerous they are."

He hurried down the stairs, and Charlotte was right behind him. Raymond was back in the house, and he could hear his mom, Reine, and Eva in the kitchen.

Marcus stepped off the bottom step, and Charlotte moved around him into the living room, over to the small desk where her laptop was.

"What's going on?" Raymond said as Marcus reached for his sheriff's jacket and lifted it from the hook.

"Marcus, I just sent the photos and files to your phone," Charlotte called out.

Marcus pulled his iPhone from his coat pocket and turned to his dad. "Can you and Mom stay?"

Raymond didn't seem surprised. He only nodded and said, "Yeah, of course. You worried about something?"

Marcus pulled out the keys to his cruiser. "Two prisoners have escaped and could be headed this way. Warden says they're dangerous, so much so that he wants us to shoot first and ask questions later, so I don't want to leave Charlotte, Reine, and the kids alone."

He knew his dad understood. "Yeah, you got it," he said. "You be careful."

Marcus thumbed through his phone and pulled up the photos his wife had sent. One was dark skinned, the other lighter, both with dark hair and brown eyes, the same bugged-out mugshot expressions. Their names were Rafe Jackson and Holter Donnelly. "Charlotte, send these to Harold and Ryan, too," he called out over his shoulder as he opened the door, and his dad was right behind him, holding the inside screen. "Charlotte has the photos," Marcus told him. "Take a good look."

Raymond nodded. "I'll call Ryan and Owen," he said.

Marcus lingered just outside. He didn't know what to say to his dad. Out of anyone, he knew Raymond had a handle on this. "Thanks," he finally said, then started down the steps. He heard the door close behind him and the lock flick closed.

He dialed his cell phone, walking straight for his cruiser and climbing in. As he tossed his duty belt and coat on the passenger seat, the phone rang once, twice…

"Okay, what did you forget?" Suzanne answered. He thought he heard Arnie fussing in the background.

"Put Harold on," he said, shoving his cell phone in the mount on the dash. He started the car.

"No can do," Suzanne said. "He's in the shower. What is it?"

There she went, playing interference. He knew she was still pissed at him because he wouldn't let her play cop in his county.

"You tell Harold to get the hell out of the shower and call me back," he said. "There was a prison break. This is serious shit, Suzanne. Charlotte just sent him the photos and files. I need him to dig into it and then meet me at the office. I'm not messing around. Have him call me. Can you do that?"

She was quiet for a second. "Don't take my head off, Marcus. Yeah, I'll tell him. Hey, big brother?" She always seemed to need to have the last word.

"What?" he said as he backed the cruiser out, ready to get off the phone. He flicked on the headlights and gave the vehicle gas, looking out into the darkness, knowing he'd be taking a second and third look at anyone he saw that night, scrutinizing who they were and what they were doing.

"Watch your back," she said.

He felt a smile tug at the corners of his lips. "Always do," he said. "Now have Harold call me."

Marcus ended the call before his sister could add one more thing. As he rounded the corner, feeling his own angst, he drove slower than usual and took a good, long look at the few pickups parked along the street, scanning for anyone out walking. There was only a couple with a dog.

This was going to be a really long night.

"Lorhainne Eckhart is one of my go to authors when I want a guaranteed good book. So many twists and turns, but also so much love and such a strong sense of family."

(LORA W., REVIEWER)

New York Times & USA Today bestseller Lorhainne Eckhart is best known for writing Raw Relatable Real Romance where "Morals and family are running themes." As one fan calls her, she is the "Queen of the family saga." (aherman) writing "the ups and downs of what goes on within a family but also with some suspense, angst and of course a bit of romance thrown in for good measure."

Follow Lorhainne on Bookbub to receive alerts on New Releases and Sales and join her mailing list at Lorhainne-Eckhart.com for her Monday Blog, all book news, give-aways and FREE reads. With over 120 books, audiobooks, and multiple series published and available at all, retailers now translated into six languages. She is a multiple recipient of the Readers' Favorite Award for Suspense and Romance, and lives in the Pacific Northwest on an island, is the mother of three, her oldest has autism and she is an advocate for never giving up on your dreams.

"Lorhainne Eckhart has this uncanny way of just hitting the spot every time with her books."

(CAROLINE L., REVIEWER)

The O'Connells: *The O'Connells of Livingston, Montana are not your typical family. A riveting collection of stories surrounding the ups and downs of what goes on within a family but also with some suspense, angst and of course a bit of romance thrown in for good measure. "I thought I loved the Friessens, but I absolutely adore the O'Connell's. Each and every book has different genres of stories, but the one thing in common is how she is able to wrap it around the family, which is the heart of each story." (C. Logue)*

The Friessens: *An emotional big family romance series, the Friessen family siblings find their relationships tested, lay their hearts on the line, and discover lasting love! "Lorhainne Eckhart is one of my go to authors when I want* *a guaranteed good book. So many twists and turns, but also so much love and such a strong sense of family." (Lora W., Reviewer)*

The Parker Sisters: *The Parker Sisters are a close-knit family, and like any other family they have their ups and downs. Eckhart has crafted another intense family drama… "The character development is outstanding, and the emotional investment is high…" (Aherman, Reviewer)*

The McCabe Brothers: *Join the five McCabe siblings on their journeys to the dark and dangerous side of love! An intense, exhilarating collection of romantic thrillers you won't want to miss. — "Eckhart has a new series that is definitely worth the read. The queen of the family saga started this series with a spin-off of her wildly successful Friessen series." From a Readers' Favorite award—winning author and "queen of the family saga" (Aherman)*

Billy Jo McCabe Mystery: *The social worker and the cop, an unlikely couple drawn together on a small, secluded Pacific Northwest island where nothing is as it seems. Protecting the innocent comes at a cost, and what seems to be a sleepy, quiet town is anything but.*

Lorhainne loves to hear from her readers! You can connect with me at:
www.LorhainneEckhart.com
lorhainneeckhart.le@gmail.com

Also by Lorhainne Eckhart

The Outsider Series
The Forgotten Child
A Baby and a Wedding
Fallen Hero
The Awakening
Secrets
Runaway
Overdue
The Unexpected Storm
The Wedding

The Friessens: A New Beginning
The Deadline
The Price to Love
A Different Kind of Love
A Vow of Love, A Friessen Family Christmas

The Friessens
The Reunion
The Bloodline
The Promise
The Business Plan
The Decision
First Love
Family First
Leave the Light On
In the Moment
In the Family
In the Silence

The Stalker
The O'Connell Family Christmas
The Girl Next Door
Broken Promises
The Gatekeeper
The Hunted

The McCabe Brothers
Don't Stop Me
Don't Catch Me
Don't Run From Me
Don't Hide From Me
Don't Leave Me
Out of Time

A Billy Jo McCabe Mystery
Nothing As it Seems
Hiding in Plain Sight
The Cold Case
The Trap
Above the Law
The Stranger at the Door
The Children
The Last Stand
The Charity
The Sacrifice

The Street Fighter
Finding Home

The Wilde Brothers
The One
The Honeymoon, A Wilde Brothers Short
Friendly Fire

Not Quite Married, A Wilde Brothers Short
A Matter of Trust
The Reckoning, A Wilde Brothers Christmas
Traded
Unforgiven
The Holiday Bride

Married in Montana
His Promise
Love's Promise
A Promise of Forever

The Parker Sisters
Thrill of the Chase
The Dating Game
Play Hard to Get
What We Can't Have
Go Your Own Way
A June Wedding

Kate & Walker
One Night
Edge of Night
Last Night

Walk the Right Road Series
The Choice
Lost and Found
Merkaba
Bounty
Blown Away: The Final Chapter
He Came Back

The Saved Series

Saved
Vanished
Captured

Single Titles
Loving Christine